SHORE
AND SHELTER

Joe is haunted by his past — his close bond with Charlie, his childhood friend; his failed relationship with Ruth; the mysteries of his pioneer great-aunt Lizzie — he knows he must understand its meaning to give purpose to his future with his wife, Sally, and their young son.

From its graphic opening scenes of the physical, masculine world of fishing boats, pubs and small coastal communities, to its gentle depictions of domesticity and family life, to the sensitive exploration of Joe's interior life, *Shore and Shelter* is a compelling and intelligent novel.

Keith McLeod was born in the south-west of Australia in 1949. He continues to live there with his wife and the youngest of their four children. *Shore and Shelter* is his first novel.

Brenda / Nice chatting in the shop. April '09 Cheers / Keith

SHORE
AND SHELTER

Just a gentle yarn!

KEITH McLEOD

Cheers
Keith
March '09.

FREMANTLE ARTS CENTRE PRESS

First published 2000 by
FREMANTLE ARTS CENTRE PRESS
25 Quarry Street, Fremantle
(PO Box 158, North Fremantle, 6159)
Western Australia.
www.facp.iinet.net.au

Copyright © Keith McLeod, 2000.

This book is copyright. Apart from any fair dealing for the purpose of
private study, research, criticism or review, as permitted under the
Copyright Act, no part may be reproduced by any process without
written permission. Enquiries should be made to the publisher.

Consultant Editor Ray Coffey.
Production Coordinator Cate Sutherland.
Cover Designer Marion Duke.

Typeset by Fremantle Arts Centre Press
and printed by Success Print, Bayswater, Western Australia.

National Library of Australia
Cataloguing-in-publication data

    McLeod, Keith, 1949- .
    Shore and shelter

    ISBN 1 86368 272 4.

    I. Title.

    A823.3

The State of Western Australia has made an investment in this project
through ArtsWA in association with the Lotteries Commission.

Publication of this title was assisted by the Commonwealth Government
through the Australia Council, its arts funding and advisory body.

To

Polly, Jack, Sull,

Ash and Connor

Acknowledgements

Thanks to Brian Dibble, Elizabeth Jolley and Tim Winton for early encouragement, to Wendy Jenkins and Ray Coffey for their editorial insight, to Danielle Haigh and Lesley Parker for the typing and, of course, thanks to Polly, for her understanding.

Although some ideas for characters and setting are from real life, the spirit and intent of this work is always towards that 'truth' created in imaginative fiction.

ONE

I have to write this for you (not that it will be like following a map to find treasure) but because I am at the beginning too, and think that in the telling I might discover what it is I need to know.

'In the telling' — already the thing sounds serious — maybe it is, and perhaps I shouldn't get too concerned about the apprehension in my voice.

I don't know where it will go; right now, as I look around, there is only the house and, outside the window, the trees with the wind blowing them. In a funny sort of way it is exciting not to have a clear plan.

I've become more settled lately, getting ready for this, I suppose, and in the last few days I've gone outside early in the morning, heard the magpie and the crow on the hill and in the valley and come back in to sit quietly while Sally slept, beginning to feel warmer, as if an old friend had come with a coat and said, 'Here, put this around you, we'll be leaving soon, it's a long way, keep yourself warm.'

It's peaceful sitting in the house early in the morning, watching the sky get lighter with the slow changing of the colours, sometimes walking in to see Sally, asleep, and then to Sonny's room and seeing the stillness of his gold-coloured hair on the pillow and his funny little drawings stuck on the wall.

I'm not going anywhere, of course, but I can't remember when I've felt closer to the scent; the idea of following it has been strong. This morning it got even stronger: I went out of the house at dawn into the cool, quiet light. A couple of kangaroos in the paddock looked up and then ignored me. I watched them for a while and then suddenly had the feeling that Charlie was standing alongside me. I looked at the dawn sky and felt that something big was about to happen. It seemed that soon the light would show what someone had been preparing: a simple stage for a simple story.

I was anchored to the light. The kangaroos looked over at me again and then went on eating and the sun rose. A velvety black crow hopped up from the ground near a big peppermint tree. It flapped and flew away, swerving once in the new sunlight.

I turned back and Charlie turned with me. Well, there was only my shadow and just one set of footprints on the dewy grass, but I swear he was there with his matted golden hair, bouncy walk and big smile.

By the time I reached the house I felt he'd slung an arm over my shoulder (he'd never done that in his life!) just to remind us both of what we could never do and what we'd been left with.

It's good to feel that he's around. It's as if he will turn and I'll follow his eyes again and see all of the fresh, untouched country. Holy Christ! Hitch your swag up Charlie! Give the world your famous smile. Pick up the cat. Have a joke with it. Sing one of your wild songs!

I'd better wake Sally soon. She needs plenty of time to get organised for work. I'll let Sonny sleep a bit longer. I could go in and whisper, 'Sonny, wake up, come out and have a talk,' but I won't. When you see him asleep, breathing quietly, you just want him to stay like that.

It would be nice to let Sally sleep, too, and then say, 'Hey! It's late. Half the day has gone. Forget about work today. Get up and we'll go for a walk down to the river.'

We've been married ten years. We married late — well, I was thirty, Sally a year younger. I suppose it's not late by today's standards.

Sonny was born five years ago. I stopped working to look after him when he was a year old and Sally went back to her job.

I was born in a little town about ten kilometres from here. So was my father. My great-grandparents on my father's mother's side came to this place over one hundred and fifty years ago. It's the same old farm. No cows these days though. No running through the paddocks in the mornings to the dairy. After the milking my father would hoist me up onto the horse with him and we'd ride back to the house.

I never knew my father's mother; she's buried not far from here in the local cemetery with my great grand-parents, but there have been stories about her and the others and I've come to have my own ideas of what they were like and how they lived.

In this part of the country the creeks run cold in the winter and the bush, folding back from the steep valleys, dries out in the summer. A bushfire will roll through the tops of the trees, with kangaroos and birds and lizards coming crazed with panic out of the smoke while the black ash floats down. People have run from the bushfires, too, but that does not happen very often.

Winter storms blow trees over the narrow roads and at the coast sand flies along the beaches while waves build and break on the rocks.

There are places at the coast where the hills slope with broken rock down to the water and waves wash into the caves. The bones of rock are sharp and it is rough going when you walk, but if you go on and follow the coast, leaving the rock bones behind, you can still hear the thump of the waves in the caves and up ahead there will be a beach, a sheltered bay, with green pools of water in the reef and fishermen's huts above the shore. (Well, when I was a kid the huts were there — they've gone now.)

This country is not always wet but even in the summer the rivers can be cold and children, after swimming, will come shivering out of the water and find warm banks to lie on and hug the sand up to their bodies. There are times, though, when the kids don't seem to feel the cold as they splash and laugh. The creeks flow white and frothing around rocks and the kids will scramble up the bank while the rains slants down through the trees.

I've often imagined what it would be like to look down from above, from high up, like an eagle. You would see the cleared paddocks and the darker lines winding through them which are the creeks and at the edge of a dark spread of bush, a farmhouse. Or you might have seen, when I was a boy, as the rain cleared and clouds blew away, four kids run wet from the trees and across the paddocks.

My brothers and sister and I would run home to the farmhouse thinking about the kitchen stove, the warm fire and eating toast. Our toy boats made from bark and sticks would be left behind, broken on the creek bank. We'd see the house with smoke coming from the chimney and going away over the trees. I'd run hard out in front with my sister, my younger brothers behind, the youngest a long way back, walking. He'd watch the ground, pull out a clump of grass, throw it away and run again.

At the house we'd push and jostle to get the best place near the stove, our hands red from the cold. Our mother would beat the cake mix with a wooden spoon. She'd already been into the small town to arrange flowers in the church to be ready for Sunday morning. I'd look out through the window, waiting to see my father who had walked to the other side of the farm to check cattle.

When our youngest brother came in our mother, knowing the look on his face, would give him the spoon to lick. He'd be happy with it, sitting on a chair near the wooden table, licking without smiling.

Outside the house were two tanks on timber stands that held the rainwater. Further away in a patch of swampy bush was a well with a windmill above it.

You could go out of the house to sit on a little porch at the front. It was a sheltered place in the sunlight on cold winter mornings. From the porch you could see across the paddocks past a split rail fence. Magpies sometimes swooped down and landed on the rails and there were places where the horses had rubbed against the wood and left hair in the splinters.

There was a door from the porch which opened into a small room with an open fireplace and a window at one side. You could jump out of the window and be on the back verandah. My brothers and I slept there on bunks and it was partly open to the weather. When the nights were wild and rain came in over the timbers and onto the beds my mother came in the dark and covered us with heavy coats.

The house had no electric light. At night a kerosene lamp burned and you pumped it to keep the pressure up. At times the lamp would block and splutter. If someone carried it to another part of the house, the rest of us would wait in the kitchen, which seemed dark at first until the glow from the fire made our shapes come back to us.

Our sister had a bedroom of her own and our parents' bedroom faced east with a big window and when there were no clouds it was full of sunlight in the mornings. A little way from the house was a shed and a woodheap with an axe stuck in a piece of wood. Past the shed, in the paddock, was a huge peppermint tree with an old cart near it. Horses pulled the cart once, but that was a long time ago when our grandparents lived here.

At night foxes came near the back of the house and got into the chookpen.

It was a long walk along a track that ran at one side of the farm to catch the school bus. The bus travelled through the big timber country, past cleared paddocks and over bridges with the fast water running below and lilies growing on the banks. We waited at the side of the road until the bus arrived and took us to the small town and the school. When my father went to school there were no buses. He rode his horse. And when his mother was a girl there were no schools here. She was taught by her oldest sister, Lizzie. Where did Lizzie learn, I wonder? Did her father come home to the little hut and put her on his knee at night after a hard day searching for cattle on the coast hills? Or maybe her mother put aside the knitting needles, turned up the flame in the lantern and said, 'Come here now Lizzie, come and look at the book with me.'

My great-aunt Lizzie began a diary when she was twenty-two. She'd write about her brothers, sisters, parents, horses, cattle, food, weather … the diary covered a three-year period with an entry for every day. She'd say:

Jan 7th, 1885. Harry went out to help cut the chaff. He rode Lucifer with a makeshift saddle and bridle.

And …

Jan 10th, 1885. I very busy, got things done up and baked and done a good day's washing down the river.

Her words would make me feel the way you do in the heavy quietness that comes after rain on a grey day and, lately, I've also started to imagine her walking back from the river with afternoon summer sun on her face. I've begun to sense sounds, light, other life, another life. I think I can see what she sees and always she is looking ahead and I am going back to meet her. And it is her words, her quiet words, making me believe in a place where the story begins; it's exciting thinking that perhaps the only story I want to tell is buried, but breathing in simple words; it's a story I have to imagine — like seeing a tiny bright flower close to the earth and then looking up and away to the faded colours of the bush, hills and distance.

But I have to leave you for now, Lizzie. You came here with your parents, bringing your Irish ways and dreams. And so this place became my father's home and mine. But it was Charlie, as I said, who came to remind me of how we left here and our first adventures together, of the shadows on the beaches and the pink light on the ranges in the north as we sailed together on the old fishing boat.

He came to me at sunrise and must have followed his shadow across hills, beaches — I don't know, but he was there and the sunlight shaking in his hair seemed to make my heavy heart roll away. Jesus Christ! Slip the ropes boys! Pull the pick! Sharpen your knives! Charlie, you've come a long way to find me. Let the hunt begin!

TWO

Charlie and I sit together on the gunwale at the stern of the seventy-foot boat as it moves north over the sunlit ocean. In another three days we should be close to the fishing grounds.

He doesn't say anything and starts picking at his toes as the boat moves steadily on through the blue, gentle lifting swells. Water from the deck hose washes over the deck and out through the scuppers. He lights a cigarette and hands his packet over to me. We smoke in silence. There is something that has come between us as we sit with the dull throb of the motor and the water bubbling out behind. We know familiar things: growing up in the south-west; our fathers and the war they went to and the farms they came back to; the wild winters and coast and the bush in the spring; the move to the north.

I sit near Charlie in silence, thinking about it, thinking about how I'd seen him five years earlier, walking barefoot with his loose swagger along the red dirt track that led to the first shop that had been built in the new town. I'd stood and watched him coming with his big hat pushed back and his dog running ahead. ('Young

Charlie's in town now,' my father had said, 'You should go and say good day to him.')

We'd tried to talk to each other, knowing that because our fathers had shared something we shared it too. He'd told me about a horse he had in a yard on the outskirts of town.

We were sixteen, the sky was blue, the sun fierce and the dirt red. It was very different to the wet country of the south and we sensed the excitement in each other. It was the start of our friendship, the beginning of horse rides along the beaches, the beginning of going further north together to drive the big machines and now we are going back to start the fishing and it is different but the same and the gentle swells lift and move into our stillness.

I look over at him, smoking, silent, watching the ocean.

'You tell your mother you're coming home?' he asks suddenly.

'Yeah. I rang her from Fremantle before we left.'

'What was happening up there?'

'Not much. She didn't say much. They'd had a bit of rain. She was happy about that.'

He doesn't say anymore.

It will be different working together on the ocean. This is Charlie's second season but it is all new for me. I wonder what he is thinking about as he flicks his smoke away. Claire, probably. Or Jane, their little daughter.

But it is strange how both our fathers are dead and sometimes, when we are silent together, it seems as if it is hard to think of anything else.

I didn't really know Charlie when we were kids. He grew up about thirty miles away. Our fathers knew each other well. They came home from the war to the place they'd been born in to run the farms and milk the cows and maybe nothing seemed the same to them: when I was a kid and saw my father tackling danger — fighting a bushfire, killing a snake, rounding up a mad bull — it always seemed to me that nothing could ever frighten him. I suppose that a barroom brawl in the local pub was never going to be very much of anything after swimming for the ships off Crete or listening to the shells and waiting for them to explode in Egypt. What those men looked for, I think — Charlie's dad and mine and others like them — was humour. They were serious sometimes, with the far-off looks on their faces and angry at other times, too, but when they got together it seemed so easy for stories and yarns and laughter to crackle all around them.

The past is close and so clear it snorts like a horse with its head reefed in hard after a gallop. I remember the night rides, flat out galloping away from the town across the spinifex with bottles of cider in the saddlebags and the horses dropping down through dry creek beds when the fear of the fall blew into us like wind and we tensed harder, lost to each other in darkness. Once, ahead, and feeling frozen without him, I pulled my horse up, my legs shaking, and heard the sound of Charlie's horse coming fast and louder on the hard ground until he wheeled to a stop and seeing me, dimly, said, 'Fuck me dead! You right mate?' We shook and laughed and our horses snorted.

The skipper comes down the wheelhouse ladder and shouts through the galley, 'Hey, Charlie. Come on. Wheel watch!' Charlie stands up, languid, brown, his gold hair matted. He balances easily to the roll of the deck, lets the water from the hose run over his bare feet, looks over at me and says, 'Fuck it, better go up I s'pose,' and walks through the galley to start his watch.

We have come from Fremantle and will sail eight hundred miles north until we reach the home of the turtles. We will do our hunting in the shallow water between the beaches and the outside reefs and around the islands and mangrove swamps where the turtles feed and breed.

There are six crewmen and the skipper; Charlie is in the wheelhouse with him now, the rest of the crew are resting. I've never killed turtles before. I've killed kangaroos and rabbits and cats. Turtles will be different. I've heard the skipper say, 'Get all the rest you can on the trip, 'cos after the first day's catch you'll be stuffed.'

Everything is ready. The knives have been sharpened, the slings spliced. The crew have made sheaths for their knives and ropes have been spliced around the shackles at the end of the harpoons. Two fourteen-foot aluminium boats are stowed and lashed amidships across the freezer hatch. If you look down from the wheelhouse you can see the hulls of the dinghies and the big black boiler on the deck — forward, port side — and the drums of outboard motor fuel jammed in above the fo'c'sle. Then, if you turn and look behind there is the superstructure, level with the wheelhouse, and a platform above the aft deck with all the cardboard sheets stacked under canvas — hundreds of flat sheets ready to be stapled together into cartons after the first load of turtles.

This is a freezer boat. The butchering and processing of the catch is done on board. Turtle skins from the flippers are packed and stacked; the red meat goes into separate boxes; the boiled jelly from the shells is sorted and stacked away in the freezer with the other cartons.

It is a narrow boat, an old boat, with the engine room throbbing below the aft deck and the wheelhouse.

The sun has gone down. The ocean is a colder dark blue. Charlie comes down the ladder and out onto the deck.

'Your watch, mate,' he says.

'Yeah. Okay.'

I go through the galley and climb the ladder to the wheelhouse.

'I'll bring you up a cuppa,' he calls after me. I glance back down at him. He is smiling. 'You want one?'

'Yeah, that'll be good.'

The wheelhouse is small, most of it taken up by the skipper's bunk. There is a chart table at the back and a shelf in front of the wheel with the compass mounted on it.

I take the wheel and hold the boat on a due north heading and it moves easily into the swells, the spray coming off the bows. Charlie comes up with the coffee and stands alongside me.

'Be there in a couple of days — get stuck into the bastards, hey?'

'Yeah.'

The skipper sits quietly on his bunk as we drink the coffee. Charlie takes the empty cups and says, 'See you later on.' He climbs down the ladder.

'Just keep her on due north,' the skipper says. It is dark now and he has the desk light on, leaning over looking at a chart. He switches the light off and I can see the red and green glow on the wheelhouse windows from the navigation lights and then Charlie, below, walking across the deck to the fo'c'sle.

After a while I realise the skipper has gone to sleep on his bunk. There is no movement on the boat now in the darkness, just the rhythmic rise and fall and the push of the hull through the water. It is strange to feel that I am in control.

The skipper moves in his sleep. There is the dull throb of the motor and the swishing slap of the ocean. I know there are cliffs away to starboard — maybe ten miles away in the dark. I've never seen them but boats have gone down on this part of the coast. I have the uneasy feeling that the cliffs might be nearer than I think, might be ranging up close and huge, but after a while I relax and feel happy and good about the trip. The gentle rolling of the boat, the soft slapping of water, lulls me into a dreamy state. I am excited and calm at the same time and stand there, barefoot in the dark holding the wheel; at times I pull it round a few degrees just to watch the compass swing, and then let the boat slip back on course.

My thoughts drift across the water to the cliffs, to a black man standing high up looking out at a strange boat. I go beyond him, where the wind blows over dry river beds with ghost gums, pale-skinned and leaning over the banks and on further, inland, to the hills black with iron and then the flat country, miles of spinifex-covered plains.

I come back to the rhythm of the boat and watch the white water fan up from the bows against the darkness. Charlie had been quiet, earlier. This will be a different kind of trip for us: he knows he will have to teach me things. It is what had come into both of us in the silence.

The breeze has strengthened and I close one of the

wheelhouse windows. The skipper moves on his bunk. It is three hours since I started my shift. I touch his leg and say, 'Hey.' He sits up quickly and looks straight ahead and then out to the west. He climbs off the bunk and stands quietly behind me and watches the compass.

'You want a cup of coffee?' he asks.

'Yeah, okay.'

I hear him below in the galley, getting the cups, lighting the stove. After a while I duck my head down and see the water boiling on the gas stove. He is out on the deck, smoking, looks up and says, 'I'll get it.' I wait and he climbs up the ladder, hands me the coffee, and takes the wheel.

'Have a spell,' he says. 'How come you went so long?'

'Was it too long?'

'Hang on a minute.' The reading light over the desk comes on. I watch him, bent over the chart. He is a big man and he moves the slide rule with thick fingers. We listen to the hushed, rushing water on the hull. He says, 'Listen, Joe. I'll tell you something. In this game you do what you have to. Nothing else. If you're told to do a two-hour wheel watch that's what you do. Not fucking three. You with me?'

I don't answer.

'You do your share of cooking, deckwork, you get out in the dinghies and catch the bastards. Unloading, packing, butchering.' He looks straight ahead over the bow. 'In other words, we work as a fuckin' team. You don't try and overdo it, otherwise you stuff up and you stuff everything else up.'

'I'll be right.'

'You won't be right. You take it easy. Okay?'

25

'Yeah.'

'Right. Go down and shake young Martin up. Get him up here.'

I leave him, cross the deck and climb down into the fo'c'sle and wake Martin. There is a faint light of the night in the small space. I can hear the others breathing, asleep.

'What's it like up there?' Martin asks. He is sitting on the bunk, legs hanging over the side. He sounds sleepy.

'It's okay. Pretty calm. Bit of wind, but we're running with it. It's not too bad.'

'Well,' he gets off his bunk. 'Better go up.'

Martin is the youngest crew member, just turned eighteen. Charlie and I had worked with him once before. He's tough and fiery and his father taught him how to box. We'd seen him in action one night at a pub when he'd flattened a bloke about twice his age. He must have sensed the way we changed towards him, because after that he seemed to want to stay with us. I wasn't surprised to find he'd tracked Charlie down and organised himself a job on the boat so we could all be together for the season. We both knew he expected a lot from us and that made us feel good to have him around, but we also knew, even at the start, I think, that there was a lot he wanted to prove.

I stretch out on my bunk and can see the stars swing and move across the square outline of the fo'c'sle hatch as the boat rises and falls. It is good to watch them while the others sleep.

I feel a bit hollow but happy, too. It has been a strange afternoon and night; the skipper hasn't bothered me. I know he's had problems on the boat before. It is dangerous work. There have been fights. Charlie has told

26

me the skipper worries about the boat going down. He thinks it is too old, not seaworthy, jinxed. He shows a cranky face to the crew but I've noticed that at the edge of his dark moods is the hint of a smile. His friendly eyes make you see it.

So I lie there, happy and quiet and excited. I'm filled with a wild kind of promise that the unknown is about to come over the dark horizon like a friendly moon.

I watch the stars, knowing it will be good to work again with Charlie. I think about how, in a fortnight, we'll go in to the jetty near the town to unload the boat and meet up again with Claire and their little girl.

Two nights before we'd left Fremantle Claire had been with us at a pub not far from the wharf. There was a dance floor and, from the bar, I'd watched her dancing, tossing her hair and smiling at Charlie amongst the swirl of bodies. After, on the street, we all walked together under the pine trees in the park and crossed the railway line and then out along the wharf to where the boat was tied up. All the boats were quiet and still on the flat water, the mooring ropes slack, trailing down from the wharf to the bollards.

'I'm going to do some shopping tomorrow,' she'd said. 'Got to buy a few things for Jane. You still sailing the day after? I'll come down to see you off.'

Charlie had bought a car, a fairly new Holden, and Claire was driving it north to meet us up there. She planned to get work in the town while we fished. She'd be able to see Charlie for a couple of days each fortnight when we brought the boat in to unload the freezer.

When we sailed two days later she was on the dock, waving goodbye, the little girl, Jane, standing beside her in the cool morning before the sun rose. Charlie was fiddling with a rope as we pulled away, trying to find something to do. I saw Claire's ruffled hair, arms tucked around each other, rocking slightly against the wind. She waved and walked slowly back along the wharf as the boat drew away. She was slender, graceful, and moved with the same kind of lightness I'd seen in Aboriginal women in the north: it was as if she was totally at ease, even in this moment of departure; it seemed the idea of belonging had curled softly into the curve of her shoulder and slightly tilted head and rested there in a dreamy sleep. A rhythmic sense of belonging to the morning, to her child, to the parting with Charlie, seemed to move with her.

A day's travel short of the fishing grounds it is hot on the deck in the afternoon sun. We are all there, except Charlie, who is in the wheelhouse with the skipper. I look up at the two of them behind the window.

The ocean is dark blue and very deep-looking and all of the sky is a lighter blue, but whiter out near the western horizon. Martin sprays himself with the deck hose, lets the water run down over his brown body and onto the red steel deck. He pushes the end of the hose out through a scupper and sits on the gunwale. The deck dries quickly. I sit alongside Ernie, who is thin and wiry and has dark curly hair.

In the shadow of the black boiler and leaning up against it, Sarge sharpens his knife. He is the biggest man on the boat and a few years older than the rest of us. He holds a sharpening steel in his left hand and floats the knife up, down, stroking lightly against it. He stops to touch the blade with his thumb and then slowly shaves a patch of hair from his arm. He is sweating and his body shines in the heat.

I watch him rub his palm across his forehead and blond, cropped hair. We are all quieter than usual. For days now, everything has been ready but there is a tension among the crew and we've started to sharpen knives again, splice more slings, check harpoon shackles and ropes. A lot of little unnecessary things are being done.

I light two cigarettes and pass one to Ernie. Martin sits on the gunwale with a harpoon resting across his knees. It is about as thick as a thumb and nine feet long, made from spring steel with a barb flattened into the point. He drags a file lightly across it.

'Can't you get a decent edge on it, mate?' Sarge asks. 'Here. I'll show you.'

'No, I'm right.'

I can see that the two of them don't like each other and have the feeling that one day they will fight.

The moment blows away in the hot air and I watch Martin, silent, turning the harpoon slowly in his hands.

I remember the time Charlie and I had been in a pub when a man was killed. The bar was crowded with men in shorts, some wearing boots, others thongs. They were miners, drivers, construction workers. It was hot. There was cursing and laughing. The floor was wet with beer. A brawl started near the door and a bloke was shoved outside. He crashed into Charlie, knocking him down across a table. Other men stormed out. There was blood and smashed glass. The fight rolled away from us. A man fell down, surrounded by legs, bodies. I saw someone jumping up and down on the fallen man's chest. The police came and the scene quietened. A woman, much older than us, came over and wanted to wipe a cut on Charlie's cheek, but he said, 'It's nothing! Leave it! I'm all right!'

I look up and notice the skipper alone in the wheelhouse and I walk down to the aft deck. Charlie is touching up his knife on the flat stone set into the bench.

'Be there in the morning,' he says. 'You can catch your first turtle, mate.'

'Yeah. Hey, you remember that woman, the night of the fight in Hedland?'

'Yeah. You tried to crack onto her, you bastard.'

'Cut it out! She was twenty years older than me.'

'Well, I woke up in the chair and there was no bugger around. Where were you?'

'Just sitting out the back talking to her.'

'Talking? What do you mean, talking?'

'Bloody talking, that's all.'

'Yeah, sure.'

I smile and don't say anything. I want him to be unsure about it.

He laughs.

'You bastard.'

He wipes the oily blade of the knife on his shorts and says, 'That was the night the Yugoslav got killed.'

In the dawn light we come in closer to follow the reef north. The reef runs parallel with the coast about a mile out from the shore for over eighty miles until the land curves sharply around at the cape and down into the gulf.

But now, in the early morning, the skipper has us sixty miles south of the tip of the cape. We'll stay close outside the reef, follow it north and enter the calmer water behind it through one of the passages. Some of the breaks are half a mile wide, others are very narrow.

Soon we see the breakers. An easterly breeze blows the spray from them. The line of the reef smokes away into the north with the swells coming in and lifting and the wind blowing back through their crests.

After an hour we reach the passage: a wide stretch of blue water with the white breakers off in the distance marking the reef again. The skipper takes the boat around, keeping to the deeper water. Charlie perches on the bow, legs hanging; the boat comes slowly in through the blue channel.

Inside the reef the water is clear and green. I can see the beaches, a mile away and the ranges behind, rising red and brown. They are covered in low scrub. Where the gorges cut through there are patches of shadow and light and small gum trees with white trunks.

We glide over a big area of sandy bottom. The boat is barely moving.

'This will do us,' the skipper shouts. 'Let her go.'

Charlie slips the turns of chain from the bollard, we heave the anchor fluke from the gunwale and the chain runs off the flaked stack and rattles through the fairlead until the anchor hits the bottom.

He feeds out extra chain, ties it off and soon the line tightens and the boat swings slowly around into the breeze. The channel is a mile away to the north. We are tucked in behind the reef in quiet water. The pale green ocean spreads away around us but in the channel it is blue and the swells fold through the gap and break white on the reef.

We are in fresh new country, about to start the killing, and I feel as I had once as a boy in the south, walking into a cleared space in the bush and finding orchids I'd never seen before.

They were delicate, on thin stems.

'Cut through them with your fingernails,' my mother had said. 'Don't pull the roots out.'

I'd squatted down and picked one. The flower was tiny and flopped and rocked like a little skull.

'Come on! Let's get these dinghies in the water.'

The skipper is edgy. The dinghies are heavy. We swing one up onto the gunwale and slide it down to splash and settle. Charlie holds a small line from the bow and ties it back to the main boat while we load the gear.

He jumps lightly down into the bobbing dinghy. 'Grab the fuel tanks, mate.' He's in a hurry to get started. I pass the first tank down to him.

'Righto, we need a couple of blokes to give us a hand with the motor. Hey Martin! Ernie!'

Martin and Ernie are loading their dinghy on the other side. They come across the deck.

The outboard motor is awkward to lift. We manoeuvre it over the gunwale and down into the dinghy, place it on the transom and screw in the holding nuts. Charlie releases the clip so the shaft and propeller swing into position under the water.

Sarge passes me the harpoon and rope. 'Here, give us that, mate.' Charlie takes it quickly and slips the loop of rope over the bollard on the harpoon deck.

'Righto,' he says, 'we need the slings, tool box ... where's the bucket? Hey Sarge, chuck the gaff down will ya?' He looks around the dinghy, checking. 'I think we're right — let's get out there.'

'Which way you heading?' the skipper calls.

'Probably go south for a start, see what it's like.'

I squeeze the fuel bulb and pull the starter rope.

'Bit of choke,' Charlie says.

The motor starts and we push clear of the main boat. I slide the gear lever forward, twist the throttle and we surge up to plane south across the wide stretch of water. The throttle handle is stiff. The dinghy bangs over the light chop on the surface. A spray of water flies off the bows and into my face. Holy Jesus, Charlie boy! Where are we bound, m'lad?

He is coiling the harpoon rope as we fly on. 'Slow her down a sec,' he shouts, and signals with his hand. He jumps up onto the harpoon deck, holding his harpoon. The deck is covered with non-slip rubber; he lays the coiled rope down between his legs, checks the shackle and stands up straight with the harpoon pointed down in front of him. He signals for more power and we speed away again. His knees bend at the thud of the swells on the hull.

We pass over white sandy country and then darker water where the bottom is covered with weed. I try to judge the depth — ten feet, perhaps. I watch Charlie and wait for any signals, not knowing what to expect. We are a long way south of the main boat now; it is a small dark shape, way back in the distance.

Charlie thrusts his arm out suddenly. I grip the throttle

hard and force it away from me and we turn sharply to the right. His arm swings back, stabbing a new direction and I pull the motor around so we turn and bank. The spray flies. The harpoon is flat across Charlie's shoulder and I follow where it points as it marks the turtle's flight under the water. Charlie bends and flows into the turns. The dinghy spins into a tight circle and out again as the harpoon sweeps an arc. Slowly the steel tip drops, Charlie rises on his toes, harpoon angled down, poised. He holds the stance for a moment, arm high up and then whips over and drives the harpoon below. I try to cut the revs and knock the motor out of gear, but we roar ahead. Something is jammed. The harpoon rope jerks tight with a bang, the dinghy skews around and I get a glimpse of Charlie as he crashes over the side and I'm jolted off the stern. I grip the gunwale. The motor is racing, propeller churning the water under my legs as the dinghy carves a tight circle. I claw my way back on board as we spin towards Charlie's blond bobbing head; he is out of sight again, but I see only his eyes as I scramble to find the stop button on the motor.

In the silence, there is a roar in my head and the slap on the hull as rings of water spread away. Charlie swims through them until he is at the boat, climbing in.

He sits with his head in his hands and says, 'Christ.'

'You okay?'

'Yeah. What the fuck happened?'

'I don't know. Throttle jammed. Cogs or linkages or something. Couldn't get it out of gear. God almighty.'

He reaches under the bow for his cigarettes and lights one.

'I missed the turtle — that's what started it. Harpoon

got stuck in a lump of coral on the bottom. Couldn't get it out. That's what the bang was when we came to the end of the line.'

He draws hard on the smoke, looks at me, raises his eyebrows.

We find the problem, a loose linkage, and fix it. Charlie straightens the bent harpoon between the bollard and gunwale, sights along it and says, 'It's okay. Be all right.'

I test the throttle. It seems free now and we move off again, slowly.

'Won't break any records today, mate,' Charlie says. 'Ah well, takes a while to get the hang of it.' He waves me out towards the reef. I glance back and see the trail of our wake and, in the distance, the beaches with the hills behind them. In front, a long way away, I can see the fine white line of breakers on the reef. My legs shake.

More than anything else I want the two of us to be a good team. It is all new and different and this is the first act, the first throw of the harpoon. You nearly fucked it up properly, I think to myself. There is nothing I can say to him.

He turns, leaning on the harpoon, graceful. 'How's the throttle feel?'

'Feels okay now.'

'Just take it steady, mate. Head out towards the reef. Should pick up a few out there.'

Two hundred yards further on in clear water, his arm swings out again. This time I can see the dark shape of the turtle swimming under the water. It is like a shadow close to the bottom, moving fast in six feet of water. I follow Charlie's signal for more speed and the bow lifts and then flattens as we begin the chase.

Charlie grips the harpoon, resting horizontally now across his shoulder. The rope is coiled, his legs braced. His right arm is high and then sweeps down. He is bent over holding the rope that angles tightly away under the water. I cut the revs, knock the gear into neutral and grab a rope sling.

'You want the sling yet?'

'No, not yet — get the gaff.'

I wait with the gaff, leaning over, trying to see the turtle. 'Very big?'

'Not bad. Fiery bugger though.' He is straining, pulling on the rope. 'Come on old feller — in you come. Come on, mate. Righto Joe, here he is.'

The turtle's head and shell bulges to the surface, the harpoon sticking out where it has cracked through the rich colours. Charlie grabs it. 'Get the gaff in where the shell joins the neck. At the back of the neck. Don't gaff the skin.'

I lean over and hit wildly at the turtle with the gaff. I hit out again and the gaff sinks into the soft flesh at the top of the shell.

'You got him? Okay, hold him there! I'll get the sling on.'

The turtle's flippers thrash the water. Charlie fights to slip each end of the looped sling around the front flippers. He hands me the rope and jerks his harpoon out. It cracks free from the splintered pattern of colours.

'Okay, let's get the bugger in.'

We grip the sling together. The gunwale dips sharply down near the water as we rock the turtle in over the side. It bangs down into the dinghy and is gasping on its back, yellow belly plate to the sun, blood oozing from the harpoon hole.

It has a hole right through the shell and with each slow breath there is a sound like a sigh as the air and blood bubble out. Charlie says, 'First one is the hardest. Come on, let's get a few more.' I rest my feet on the turtle's firm yellow belly plate and slip us into gear.

There is a pool of blood sloshing around my feet. I bail with the bucket and the blood splatters out on the green water. I stop the dinghy and shift the turtle to trim the balance of weight. Charlie turns to watch, leaning on the harpoon.

The turtle dries out in the sun. I splash some water and its head lifts for a moment and sags back again. Clear fluid runs slowly from the eyes. The neck is leathery, old and furrowed. The turtle's face looks like a wise but tired old man.

Ahead of us the ocean floor slants up to meet the reef and we skim over the shallow water. Clumps of coral jut to the surface. A crop of staghorn coral like hard white branches spreads out under the water. There are no turtles out here. We are too close to the reef. Charlie waves me back towards the deeper water.

The next turtle is swimming over a weed bank. We have him in the boat quickly. After two hours there are seven turtles in the dinghy and it feels heavily settled as I steer north for the main boat, about three miles away. We are low in the water. I lean against the motor and bail out the mix of water and blood. Charlie sits on a turtle's belly and lights a smoke. He is relaxed now and studies his toes.

'Pretty good load,' he says.

'Couldn't get any more on, could we?'

'Oh, you'd get a couple more. Don't want to sink the

bugger on the first trip though. You seen the other dinghy?'

'They stayed south of us — still down there, I think.'

It is a slow trip back. The motor works hard and the dinghy is heavy. The turtles bleed and take long, deep breaths. They are dying slowly under the hot sun. Charlie dips the bucket over the side and splashes water on them and some over his head. He looks at me and then away.

Charlie stands on the harpoon deck as we near the main boat, ready to take the rope and tie up. Sarge and the skipper are waiting.

Unloading is heavy work. We pull the turtles to one side and pass up the sling. 'You right?' the skipper asks. He heaves on the rope with Sarge while we hold a back flipper each and shove the turtle up until it skids over the gunwale and drops down onto the steel deck.

When the last one is unloaded I jump up to fill the two fuel tanks from the drums. Sarge and the skipper have already started the butchering.

Charlie goes to the galley and comes back with a few slices of bread. I pass the fuel down to him. He unties the dinghy and away we go again.

A mile south we pass the other dinghy heading back. They are low in the water.

'They've got a good load,' Charlie says.

We hunt all day until the sun is low and it is hard to see the shadows, which are really the turtles, passing under the darkening water.

'I'm stuffed,' Charlie says, as we bring our last load in.

I feel as if I have worked a lot of things out: how to

smoothly cut the angles at the height of the chase and make subtle speed changes anticipating direction. I have worked out a way to zig-zag the dinghy so the blood and water sloshes up into a corner of the hull where I can bail it easily.

We follow the reef north with eight turtles stacked high — mounds of yellow bellies. There is a pink tinge on the water all the way across to the shore and the beaches are white against the rising hills behind. Where the gorges split the range the rocks seem alight like fire.

Martin and Ernie have finished hunting for the day and their dinghy bobs at the end of a rope behind the main boat.

Twenty-seven turtles have been caught in seven hours. There are fifteen on their backs on the deck and the crew are butchering them. We unload and I drop the dinghy back to tie up for the night. I check it over, tidy up the slings, splash some water around to clean up the blood.

When I get back the crew are bent over, barefoot, working without shirts. The skipper says, 'Righto, Joe. Over here, I'll show you how it goes. Grab that turtle. We'll work on two of 'em together. Okay? Right.'

He scrapes his knife over the sharpening steel. 'Give your knife a touch-up. If your knife's blunt you'll get cut. Now, you start here, top of the belly plate,' and he plunges his knife into the turtle and waits, watches me. 'Yeah, that's it, push it right in. Now, run it around the edge. You're away.'

I slide my knife through and all the way around the edge of the yellow shell. Warm blood runs on the deck. The skipper is at my shoulder, watching. 'Okay. Right. Now lift up an edge of the belly plate. Get your knife under it. Hold it flat and scrape along the inside of the plate. That's it. She'll come away.'

I hack with my knife. The belly plate comes away and I throw it on the heap with the others. The turtle is opened up now; all tubes and fat and blood and red meat.

The skipper wipes his forehead with the back of his hand, smearing blood. 'Righto, Joe. Now the two shoulders. Cut down about here' — his hand and knife disappear into the pool of flesh — 'there's a little bony knuckle here, you gotta get through it. Bit lower, yep, twist your knife into it. Right. Give it a good pull.' He twists and pulls as he speaks, 'and out comes your shoulder.' He tosses the heavy lump of red meat into a stainless steel vat on the deck.

'You right Joe?'

'Yeah.'

Yes, I am right. I am right to follow all the moves of his knife and right to drive it in deep and carve and tear a red shoulder of meat out and toss it into the vat then straighten up to sharpen my knife, looking casually across the water to the hills and back, seeing the others all bent and blood-spattered in their quiet fury of work and I was right as a boy, too, smacking the kittens over the head with a lump of wood and when Charlie looks at me, wrestling out a pile of ropey turtle guts I am right to ignore him even if his eyes say, 'Ah well, fuck you then,' but when it is over and we sit on the deck for a break before the boning starts, with the ocean darker now and only a faint blush of pink light in the sky above the ranges, I take the cigarette he has lit and gives to me with his bloody hand.

We begin the boning and it is another hour before we

eat. Sarge has cooked turtle stew. We sit around on the stern deck, behind the galley. There is not a lot of talking, only the sounds of hungry eating.

Later, in the fo'c'sle, the skipper pokes his head through the hatch. We are all on our bunks.

'I'll call you at five in the morning to unload the boiler and clean the shells.'

No one answers.

'You watch that sunburn tomorrow, Martin. Wear a hat.'

The fo'c'sle has six bunks built into the space at the boat's bow, under the deck. It is very cramped.

'You get sunburnt, mate?' Charlie asks, looking at me, less than an arm's length away as we lie on our bunks.

'No, I'm okay.'

'I'm burnt under the arms — fuckin' sore — have a look at this.' He shows me the red colour around his armpit.

'How'd you get burnt under there?'

'Sun shines back up off the water. Hey! How much we make today?'

It is just like him, really, to ask me that, but I'm surprised and so is Martin, who glances at me from his bunk. Charlie is no good at anyone talking about his own pain for very long, but maybe it is more than that, too. He wants to bring me in, take some control, work things out. All day I've followed his lead, watched him making directions … crew members get paid seventy cents a turtle — it's a simple sum.

'Nearly twenty bucks,' I say.

'Not bad for half a day,' he says. 'Get a full day at 'em tomorrow and we'll kill the pig'.

41

He looks at his hands, flexing them.

'Bloody hands are sore, rope burns. Take a week for them to harden up.' He lies down, pulls the rug up. 'I'm rooted mate, gotta get some sleep. See you in the morning.'

I want to sleep, too, but can't. My eyes sting from the salt water. The stars float across the hatch as the boat gently swings on the anchor and there is the slapping of water on the hull.

In the dim starlight I can see Charlie's arm hanging over the side of his bunk and can hear him breathing. When I close my eyes I can see him again, balanced, flowing, rising on his toes to throw the harpoon and I can see myself, fighting hard to hold the dinghy steady, fighting to put him exactly where he wants to be. Goodnight Charlie.

I roll over and lay still, wanting the boat to rock me into sleep and, when it does, I dream of climbing — slipping, sliding, on pale hills of raw meat.

THREE

When Sally was leaving for work this morning I gave Sonny his school bag, ruffled his hair and then watched the car drive away and went back into the house, made a coffee and took it out and sat on the verandah.

The dog saw me and ran over, wanting to play, shaking one of Sonny's old shoes in her mouth.

I drank my coffee and took the cup in and put it on the sink with the rest of the dishes. The place was a bit of a mess. Maybe today I can clean it up, I thought, and have it looking nice when Sally gets home, but I left everything and went out again to the verandah. The dog had dropped the shoe and was lying down over near the fence in the sunlight.

I sat there for nearly an hour as the shadows shrank slowly back towards the peppermint trees, then walked into our bedroom, opened a drawer and took out my great-aunt Lizzie's diary.

Her parents had come to this part of the South-West in 1859. Lizzie was born a couple of years later, the second child. By the time she started her diary in 1885 there were nine children. Often she was left in charge of the younger ones for weeks while her parents and the older boys were away trying·to establish other small holdings.

I liked going back to her simple entries and the way they made you slowly understand what it all must have meant for her. I suppose she wrote at night, in the little hut with a nib dipped in ink and a flickering lantern.

I walked out to the verandah and sat on a chair.

May 18th, 1885. Mr Curtis came up and got about 20lb flour, 1lb tea and a bit of sugar, also bottle of cough drops for little baby. Agreed to let Father have a steer today if we don't find Tinker.

May 19th. Wet day. Cut up and salted the pig. Rained very heavily.

May 21st. Minnie and Bella helping Robey dig potatoes. I busy at new suit of clothes for Willie.

May 22nd. I finished the suit, done a good job cleaning up and ironing. Father came home about 3 o'clock riding Smiler. They lost Armstrong's horse. James rode him down last Saturday and let him out at Boranup, but he got out of the paddock, has looked for two days but could not find him.

I'd read it all before, but wanted to have her sentences ring out again, slow and clear like an axe at a tree down in the valley. I loved the way she casually mentioned Armstrong, the man she loved and would later elope with. And James, her older brother ... I knew what was coming with James.

May 24th. Robey got the bullocks and some calves and other cattle branded and drove the cattle all together up on the coast hills. I finished a skirt for Mother and some other things. Packed them up in a little box.

May 28th. Got a long letter from Mother and one from James — will be in early next week, has only found seven head of our cattle.

July 31st. Wet morning. I baked and done some weeding in the garden. Robey came riding old Chips. Terrible news. Poor James is dead at the Margaret through a gun which got wet and would not go off so he put it near the fire one barrel went off so he rushed to pull it away when the other charge lodged in his head killing him instantly. Harry chanced to be with him camped at the ten mile brook cattle hunting up the river. About 8 o'clock yesterday it occurred. They had to carry him on a stretcher for ten miles.

August 1st. We made a very early start, Mr Armstrong riding his cart·horse. Father terribly upset and Robey too. We spent a most miserable day. Funeral was well attended. At 4 o'clock in the evening we saw the last of poor James.

I sat looking down at the valley and the dark trail of trees lining the creek.

Did you go back to the cold house Lizzie and stoke the smoking fire and see a campfire on a riverbank with grey paperbark trees dripping? Was James squatting, warming his hands? Did you see the gun on the ground and the ducks, flying low over the river, veer off sharply with the blast?

Sitting there, thinking about it, made me want to put something in my own diary; it wasn't a diary really, more like an old book I'd jot stuff in from time to time, thoughts, ideas, that sort of thing ... maybe something funny that had happened, something Sally had done or Sonny had said. There were huge gaps in it — there'd be times I didn't enter anything for months, or even a year. But I'd had it for a long time, even on the boat with Charlie. I used to worry back then, well, not really I suppose, but it didn't feel right, somehow, scrawling away in a book at night when Charlie would give me his glance, making me feel that he was thinking that I was writing down secret thoughts about him ... I don't know what he really was thinking, of course, but that's the way his look would make me feel.

Anyway, sometimes wanting to write in it is like speeding in a car on your way to meet someone you can't wait to be with, so I went inside and got it and came out and wrote:

Not doing a lot today — just thinking about my story and reading some of Lizzie's stuff.

Sometimes think I'm so close to making the story decent, but never really sure ...

It needs to have ... well, a lot more than it's got, needs answers I suppose. But I don't know them yet. That makes it tricky.

What I'd like to do is make it warm — light a whole string of little fires so the reader could just go from one to the next — like walking out into the night and seeing a small glow and reaching it and finding a group of

*people warming themselves, telling jokes, singing
songs.*

*I want the reader to hang around for a while and join
in and then move on again into the darkness and
further out towards the next flickering light.*

*But that's all dreamy stuff, I suppose, and what it
needs is to find out what's going on with Sally and me
and if it really is all just imaginary; I mean, Sally
might be right: it might all be just in my head for
Christ's sake! And in the end you can only imagine so
much and then you start chasing shadows. Jesus!
Punching at shadows!*

When Sally came home from work, the dog barked. I
looked through the window and saw Sonny getting out of
the car.

I walked over to the sink to make a start on the dishes.
Sonny ran in, threw his bag down and opened the fridge.

'How was it?' I asked.

'What?'

'School?'

'Every time do you have to ask that? Have we got any
biscuits?'

'Don't think so.'

He found an apple and walked across the room, biting
into it.

Sally came through the door with her briefcase. She put
it down on the kitchen table, switched the kettle on and
said, 'What have you been doing?'

'Not much.'

I couldn't tell her I'd been going back over it all again.
Not yet. I didn't know where things would go ... with

Sally, I mean; or with any of it I suppose: wandering off with Lizzie and Charlie was easier and clearer but if I'd tried to explain that to Sally she'd have said, 'Why do you need to go over all that old stuff again? Half of it's just in your imagination. You can't change anything.' And she's probably right, too, but it seems I have no choice. It's as if Charlie has walked away, turned to look back and called me with his eyes.

Charlie is shaking me. 'Wake up mate.' The light is on in the fo'c'sle. There is a banging above us on the deck. The rest of the crew are moving about, getting dressed. I sit on my bunk for a moment. My hands are stiff and sore. I pull on a jumper and pants and climb the ladder to the deck.

The skipper has the lid off the boiler and is leaning over it, steam rising above him. He pulls out a turtle shell and plucks a string of soft rubbery jelly from it. 'Yep. She's cooked. A good boil too.'

A strong wind is over the water from the south-east. The crew is coming to life. They look groggy and tired. The skipper calls out, 'Here, get these gloves on. This stuff is bloody hot.' He is unloading the boiler, tossing the cooked shells down into red baskets. Steam rises. We pull on our gloves and a basket of hot shells is upended onto the table. We pick the bones from the jelly and toss them over the side of the boat. 'She's a good boil,' Charlie says, flicking a star-shaped bone over his head and out into the black ocean. 'It's a bastard when it's not cooked properly, can't get the shell out.'

Martin says, 'What'd you say they use this stuff for, cosmetics?'

'Yeah, something like that. Gets exported anyway.'

Charlie holds a bone with a long strip hanging from it. 'Hey, watch this.' He shakes the bone and the hot strip drops to the table. 'That's the way you want it, so the bones just shake out.'

We work for an hour in the dawn light. The sun comes up over the ranges. Sharp chopping swells move alongside the boat. The wind is roughing up the swells, which seem to be racing each other.

'Gunna be a bit of a mongrel out there today,' Ernie says.

The skipper looks at the ocean. 'That's only tame, only chop, it's not real swell. You'll be right. Might get banged around a bit.'

There is no splash when the bones are thrown and hit the water — the wind makes too much noise.

'How we going? Ready for the last lot?'

Ernie has climbed into the boiler and scooped the last shell into a red basket.

'Yeah, let's get it finished.'

'The wiring machine's down the back. Grab it, will you Martin,' the skipper says. 'Bring the cartons too. They're all made up.'

The soft jelly is packed, wired tight, weighed and passed down into the freezer. The sun is higher now and shadows slope down from the ranges.

Sarge has been in the galley cooking porridge. The crew sit on the stern deck eating, while the hard wind makes the dinghies jump at the end of their ropes like snapping dogs.

'You blokes do the first trip in close to shore today,' the skipper says. 'Get a bit of shelter in there.'

The wind is blowing broken water from the low swells

as they chop past the boat. Out at the reef the line of breakers is blurred. In the south a haze is over the horizon.

'She'll swing into the north-west later and then you can fish out near the reef.'

Martin looks at the skipper. 'That's from the south now.'

'Nah, it's offshore. Look out here behind us. Stern of the boat towards the reef. Offshore.'

Charlie is ready to go. 'Tell you what Joe, we might check out the sandhills today. Any turtle with brains will be hiding up there.'

Sarge stands on the deck and watches as we motor away. White sheets of spray rise from the bows.

My eyes sting from the salt spray and I'm soaking wet. The dinghy bangs along and the water flies back over us. Charlie signals to slow down. 'Think I saw something,' he shouts. He waves me on and into a turn. The dinghy ploughs through it. Charlie wipes his eyes. The harpoon is up. He rises high with a steep swell, drops down into the trough, the harpoon wet black across his shoulder. Water smashes and flies up over him as he flows with the wild moves of the boat and the ocean.

I cannot see the turtle, but imagine it swimming deep, front flippers powering over weed and sand, water streaming across the humped shell, back flippers swinging parallel to steer wide of a coral lump. For a moment, I think this turtle has a good chance to escape, but when I look at Charlie with his free-standing balance, flowing smoothly, moving always with the dinghy like a horseman leaning into the ride, I know the odds are probably in our favour.

Charlie is on his toes. The dinghy falls into a trough, stops, settles. It swings side on and rocks in the swell. 'Hey, have a look at this.' He's pulling the rope in.

'What's wrong with him?'

'Killed him outright. Hardly ever happens. You hit 'em in a certain spot just back from where the shell meets the neck and it just paralyses them.'

He pulls the turtle close to the dinghy, jerks the harpoon out. I hold the turtle easily. It is perfectly still, as if frozen. We pull it in and it lies, cold-looking, at my feet as Charlie waves me on and I twist the throttle.

I feel cold too. The ocean is wild. The dinghy bangs into the chop and broken sheets of water spray hard into my face. It is like a south-west winter's day when you run through a driving rain shower to shelter under a tree, hugging the trunk while the wind tears at the branches.

Charlie turns and looks at me, shakes his head, smiles, his face shining wet. I watch him through the spray, my bare feet resting on the hard smooth shell of the dead turtle.

There were days in the south when I'd been out on the farm with my father and we'd sheltered under trees as rain swept up the valley and I'd seen the distant, dreaming look on his face while we waited for the storm to pass. Where did he go with that look? As a boy, I always thought he'd gone back to a place in the war. Maybe a trench in North Africa where he saw, as the dust cleared, a dead mate's body begin to take its final shape. Or perhaps he was swimming again for the ships off the beaches of Crete. I'd heard the stories, but never really knew. Did the ocean light up from the flash of shells or did he find the nets in darkness and climb, heavily, until he fell onto the broken, burning deck?

When I was a child his dreaming face always triggered an explosion of war scenes for me. I'd see flames and two ships coming together and drifting apart and men waiting for the right moment and others leaping and falling into darkness.

Charlie turns again and shouts, 'How you going back there?' He is soaked. We both are.

'Great. Nice and cosy. You spotted any mermaids yet?'

He laughs, 'You look like a shag on a rock. We'll stay …'

We fall down a swell and a thick curtain of water rips back into my face. It is like someone slapping me and shouting, 'Hey, wake up you dreamy bastard!'

'What did you say?' I yell.

'If we stay south for a while we can come home with the wind.'

For twenty minutes we zig-zag in long tacks into the south; south-east, back to north-west, south-east again, staying just wide of the full force of the wind so we ride easier over the swells and ship less water.

There are no turtles and then, swinging west towards the reef, Charlie makes a signal I haven't seen before; he shapes his hand like a claw, opens and closes it, fingers spread wide. I follow his signals, his eyes, his body, and we move north. Now, running with the swells, it is easier for me to see. We are over sandy bottom. The water is green.

The harpoon is up on Charlie's shoulder. I follow

directions from its shifting point. We cut a loop back into the south and then north again, closing in. Sometimes the harpoon drops a little, Charlie's eyes follow it and then up again, level. His face is tense, wet. He rises high. I can see nothing under the water. He throws. The rope comes tight in a second, before I am ready, and reefs the dinghy around in a half circle. I think, for a moment, we have hit something big.

Charlie falls into the dinghy, sprawling. I fight with the motor, trying to keep the propeller clear of the harpoon rope. There is a heavy bump under the hull. I slip the motor out of gear. Water spills in over the gunwale.

Charlie says, 'Big tiger.'

'Big what?'

'Shark. Tiger shark. Let the bugger tow us.'

The shark drags the dinghy through the water, the harpoon breaking the surface like a crazy periscope. It turns and I see for the first time the long grey shape coming straight for the dinghy, pushing fast under the swirling green.

'Jesus! Hang on!' Charlie shouts.

There is a bang and the big head is up, half out of the water, biting at the gunwale. Teeth scrape and splinter, the shark rolls away with a jerk and the harpoon rope is slack.

'He's off, harpoon's pulled out. Come on!' Charlie leaps to the deck, reefs the rope in hand over hand, working fast, watching and pointing. He rises and falls as we chase. I can see the grey shape again. We roar up to it. Charlie throws. 'That's a beauty, mate, I got him good and hard.'

The shark tows us steadily and we watch and wait.

There is nothing we can do until he tires. I look over all of the wind-blown water to the calm hills, two miles away. Charlie reaches under the harpoon deck for his smokes. He bends his head down between his legs to light one and, seeing the speed of the water past the dinghy, says, 'He's just about stuffed.'

He stands up on the harpoon deck and pulls the dinghy along the rope to the shark. Blood spreads away near the grey head. It is bright red in the water. The shark rolls and thrashes and the harpoon hits the gunwale.

'Get a sling ready. We'll get one round his tail in a minute.' Charlie pulls us closer.

The shark looks longer than the dinghy. Charlie holds the harpoon — the shark rolls at the end of it.

'I'll shove his head down, see if you can get the sling around his tail.'

I try to push the curved tail fin through the loop. The shark thrashes and settles again. I slip the sling over and pass the free end to Charlie.

'Here. You got it?'

'Yep. Get a couple of turns around the bollard.'

We pull the sling up to the bollard and tie it off short. Charlie twists his harpoon out of the shark's head.

I steer the dinghy north, towing the shark. The tail breaks the surface at the bow and the head hangs at the stern, wallowing heavily. The clear water flows over the dull tiger stripes around the thick body.

Charlie is relaxed now. He lounges over the harpoon deck. 'S'posed to drown them, towing them backwards.' He rubs his foot on the grey tail. 'Hate to get swiped with it, give you a bit of gravel rash.'

The skipper and Sarge are standing on the deck as we come closer. The skipper says nothing until we tie up and then walks slowly over to the gunwale and looks down.

'What the fucking hell you two think this is? We're here to catch turtles, not stuff around with sharks. And why drag the bastard back here anyway? If you want the bloody jaws cut his head off out there.'

He waves to some distant part of the ocean and walks away.

'He'll calm down,' Charlie says. 'Let's get the head off this feller.'

I gaff the dead shark's head and hold it up in the water while Charlie leans over, cutting through it with his knife. His hand and the knife blade work into the widening split and the big head sags away from the body. I swing the gaff into the head again, rolling the shark.

Charlie slashes under the water and the head comes off and hangs on the gaff as the grey body swings away. He slips the rope from the tail and the shark slides down through the green water to the bottom.

'See this?' Charlie has the jaws open, pointing at the teeth with his knife. 'See all the rows of teeth, knock a couple out and the new ones just fold down to take their place.'

There are some broken teeth. 'That's where he snapped at the gunwale. Better sling this up on the deck and head out again.'

The skipper returns. 'Good size shark. Listen, grab a coffee before you get back out there again. I've made some, down in the galley.'

We sit in the galley, having a break, and drink our coffee.

'Told you he'd come good,' Charlie says, holding the big mug, both hands around it, his mouth barely leaving the rim.

We push off from the main boat and thump across the chop towards the reef, passing Martin and Ernie. They come out of the shine of sunlight on the water and are close before we see them.

We hunt for four hours in the shallow waters near the reef; it is sheltered from the wind. When we arrive back with our load the skipper says, 'That'll do fellers, it's been one of those days — bit windy — makes it hard. We'll clean this lot up and hit 'em again tomorrow.'

Later, as we sit around eating our meal, he says, 'Fifty a day is good going, you get down around the twenty mark and your average drops. You get under that and it's fuckin' hard to push it up.'

'Was bloody rough out there today,' Martin says. 'Plenty of turtles but too rough to catch the buggers.'

'If that wind drops we'll get fifty tomorrow,' Charlie says, sitting on the deck, the shark jaws between his legs. He doesn't look up as he speaks and trims thin sinews of flesh from the jaws with his knife. He studies a strip of meat he's cut, flicks it over the side of the boat and adds, 'Maybe even a hundred.' We are all watching the way he cuts and trims the jaws.

Ernie stands up. 'Gunna fuckin' play cards or not?'

'Yeah, let's go.'

The wheelhouse is a cramped area to play cards in; a couple of us sit on the skipper's bunk, the others lean back against the chart table and the wheel.

'Sarge playing?'

'He's reading. Leave him, he's happy.'

We play blackjack. Someone wants to play poker but the skipper says, 'We're playing fuckin' blackjack,' and deals the cards.

The wind has dropped and the boat hangs steady. The skipper holds the pack. 'What are you doing?'

'Sitting.'

'Joe?'

'Buy.'

He passes a card and I slip it in with my hand. 'Okay, I'll sit.'

We play for fifteen minutes and the skipper holds the deal and wins. Martin turns up a blackjack and takes over the deal. On the first hand he says, 'Pay seventeens.'

Ernie and I collect. The skipper quietly returns his cards.

'What'd you sit on?' Ernie asks. There is no answer. 'You sat on sixteen, you bastard,' Ernie says and laughs. 'He always sits on sixteen. You can bank on it.'

I look at the skipper. He's in control, almost smiling, and is holding the cards tightly behind his hand.

When the game finishes I linger down on the stern deck. Charlie fiddles with the shark jaws. They look clean and white. He has them held open into a wide yawn with a piece of timber jammed between the top and bottom rows of teeth.

'They look good,' I say. 'Do you want a coffee?' He picks at the jaws again with his knife, concentrating hard, and doesn't answer. 'I'll go and make one.'

I make two coffees and carry them out from the galley. It is a clear night. The Southern Cross swings bright above the dark water. We can hear the waves somewhere out behind us, breaking on the reef. Charlie holds the jaws up. 'What do you reckon?' He is smiling, his head inside the jaws, ropey blond hair dry and matted.

'A work of art.'

He puts the jaws on the bench and stands looking at them.

We sit on the gunwale, drinking the coffee and smoking. Charlie reaches over and cuts a length of cord from a reel hanging at the side of the bench and starts twisting it in his fingers, tying little slip knots and flicking them open.

'What have you got planned for the end of the season?'

He looks up quickly. 'Haven't thought about it,' he says, 'Bit early yet.'

'Think you'll go back driving? On the machines?'

'Maybe, it's either that or get onto another boat somewhere.'

I flick my smoke away. 'Might go down and get some sleep.'

'Yeah,' Charlie says, 'I won't be far behind you.'

I lie in the dark little cave of the fo'c'sle with the lighter rectangle of sky above me. It feels good to stretch out and relax. I squeeze my eyes tightly shut and they are moist and stinging from the salt when I open them.

I try to think of nothing, so I can sleep, but know it won't work and, anyway, the peaceful rocking in the fo'c'sle at night is something I love. It is easy to drift away.

I think about the women of the cool south, women wearing long dark dresses, moving like shadows in old houses. They take the black kettle from the stove to make tea for my father while his horse stands outside, waiting in the rain. They reach up into a thick jar on the shelf above the fireplace and hand me a biscuit. Lizzie's sisters. My dad's aunts. I never saw Lizzie, of course. She'd been dead for years. My grandmother died when I was a baby. But the other sisters were alive and moved through my childhood like shadows in their long dark dresses.

They were different from my mother, who seemed young and colourful. The older women never seemed to come out of the houses. As a boy I believed the dark house — the stove, the shadows, the old wooden floors, the small rooms with heavy doors — had grown around these women like a black night settles around birds in quiet trees.

I lie on my bunk and think about what they must have been like as girls and young women: I see them riding side-saddle along the tracks with splashes of sunlight falling between the big trees; stooping to drink from clear flowing creeks on hot days; splashing water on a horse to cool it; caught out in a shower of autumn rain; stopping on the coast hills to look at an orchid; and in the war, wondering and waiting.

There were no cars when Lizzie was a girl. When I was a boy it was different. We'd go in the car to the little town and into the tiny church. And the women of the town would be there in their best Sunday clothes. This was my mother's generation, singing hymns in their hats and gloves. They'd sing on Sunday and come home to farmhouses to swing an axe and cart wood down to the kitchen stove, their arms scratched from the rough bark and little black ants crawling on their skin.

I wonder if they might have swum naked in rivers or

walked naked in quiet shaded parts of the bush. Would they really have done that? Would they have wanted to shock some part of themselves into the smooth flow of a dark river? I don't know. I only see them turn, walking on a bush track, to say to a child, 'Come on, I've got bread in the oven.' And the child, running, catching up, holding wildflowers, saying, 'Look at these.'

I remember the flowers arranged in glass vases in the church and watching the priest light the candles and drink wine and talk in swollen tones about sin and goodness and love. I remember women in church holding a finger to their lips to silence children and my father's dreamy face as the priest spoke.

I think about my father as a younger man, before he brought us to the north. Whenever I remember him in this way I put him into places of peace, moments of silence. I see him on a rock near the river with a lizard close to his feet. Perhaps he raised one foot slowly as if it would appeal to the lizard and said, 'You go away now and get some rest, go under a rock.' The lizard, steady, silent, with just the flutter of breathing under the chin. My father's hands loose and calm.

I see him looking up into the first bend of the river where the banks come steeply up with trees and branches hung over the dark water and then going further, past the curve of sandhills and on across the beach with the river breaking out shallow into the ocean. And then, returning to the silence of the rock, the lizard gone. Rising to walk slowly back across the paddocks and into the farmhouse where my mother sat sewing, so calm and quiet that it would be false for him to say, 'I talked to a lizard — he had the speed of sunlight, the silence of rock.'

I don't know, of course, if he ever sat on that rock and talked to the lizard. It's true, though, that he knew the place, took me there with him on horseback, but it was always part of something else: checking a fence on the far side of the farm near the river or looking for a stray cow. He was a man of action really, but there was also a look which came over his face that made me want to follow his thoughts to see what he saw. Anyway, what does it matter? I can't ask him now. That's another curious thing Charlie and I share: both our fathers came away from the south as if wanting to find light, warmth and excitement; both brought their families with them to the heat and the red dirt; and then the two of them, within months of each other, died. They died in a place a long way from the cool south.

Sometimes it is with us, this feeling of sharing: fathers who went to war and came home and left their homes again to find the dry heat of the north. It is with us in silence.

Charlie's father was a gentle man. I remember a day when we'd ridden back to his place from the yards out of town. The horses were tied to a scrubby tree, flicking their tails as we sat together having a beer. Charlie's father looked at them and said, 'When I was a kid the wild horses would come out at dusk. They had a leader, you know, and he'd take them up the hill and just stand still up there or turn his head sometimes and look out at the other hills. Beautiful animal.'

The nights on the bunk take me away from my tired body. I think of Claire and the little girl, Jane, and how they might be waiting on the jetty when we come in to unload the boat. Perhaps she'll see the boat a long way off and she'll say to her daughter, 'Here they come,' and watch as the white bow wave gets clearer, the boat gets closer, until she can see us getting ready with the ropes and Charlie will toss the rope onto the jetty and jump down and tie it around the bollard and then turn to watch them walk along the planks towards him.

For five days Charlie's set of shark jaws dries in the sun on top of a fuel drum. Three hundred turtles have been caught and processed, the last hundred in two days at new grounds after the skipper moved the boat ten miles north one morning and came through a narrow passage to anchor inside the reef.

It is late afternoon. In the morning we'll make the trip up around the cape and down into the gulf to anchor off the beach and spend the night in the town. The following day we'll take the boat further south to unload at the jetty.

We're taking a break from butchering the last of the day's catch. Charlie looks north at the ocean and the darker, blurred line in the distance where it meets the land.

'Be home tomorrow, mate,' he says.

'Yeah.'

'Your mum knows you're coming?'

'Yeah, she knows.'

'She'll be happy,' he says.

The skipper shouts, 'Hey c'mon, let's get these done so we can clean the boat.'

Martin says, 'Get into it Charlie, but don't work too hard. You'd better take it easy. Save your strength. You reckon she'll be waiting?'

'Dunno,' Charlie says. 'If she is I'll keep her out of your bloody reach.'

In the morning, before daylight, the skipper shouts down through the fo'c'sle hatch, 'Come on, you lazy bastards, time to pull the pick.'

We come up the ladder, pushing hair from our eyes, looking out at the calm water and the red glow of the dawn sky over the hills. The skipper laughs, 'Bloody lively looking mob. Go and grab a quick cuppa. We'll need two blokes to do the anchor and a couple to keep an eye on the dinghies.'

After the coffee we are properly awake and keen to get the anchor on board and be on our way.

'Let's get her up, boys,' Martin says, throwing his cup into the big plastic washing-up drum. 'Be in the fuckin' pub tonight if we get moving.'

Sarge has two turns of chain around the winch drum as it slowly revolves and, for the first time, I flake the chain as it comes steadily off the drum. I flake it into a square stack on the deck, running lengths in one direction for a layer and then back at right angles for the next.

Ernie leans over the gunwale and signals the direction of the chain out under the water and the skipper idles the boat slowly forward. Martin and Charlie stay at the stern to keep the two dinghies from banging together.

The anchor leaves the bottom and comes straight up through the green water and breaks the surface. Ernie reaches over. 'Give us a hand here for a sec.'

I help him twist a heavy anchor fluke so it rests over the gunwale. Sarge ties the chain around the bollard, the skipper swings the wheel and the boat comes around and moves slowly out towards the gap in the reef.

Ernie stays at the bow 'spotting' for dark patches. It is a cool morning. He wears a coat and has pulled a woollen cap down over his ears. The skipper watches from the wheelhouse, his hand lightly on the wheel.

Most of the dark patches are weed, but in places lighter shaded lumps of coral rise up from the bottom. When the water breaks and washes over them they are easy to see, but the lumps down deeper, a few feet under the surface, have to be 'spotted' and cleared. The signal and shout comes from Ernie on the bow: 'Hard to starboard, fifty yards ahead.'

When we reach the deeper water of the passage there is a surge of revs and we sail out through the break in the reef. I watch the two dinghies towing along in our wake. Far away, behind them, are the beaches and hills. I look back to where we'd been anchored, probably a mile away now in the calm green water, and think about the bones left behind and the grey, headless shark.

The boat pushes out into the deep blue and swings to starboard, and I can see the swells inside us lift and break onto the reef.

For an hour we follow the reef north until the tip of the cape curves around. The lighthouse is high on the craggy sprawling range.

We cut in close to the land and can see the dark rocks on the beaches, the waves washing up the shore and lighter slabby yellow rocks higher up.

'There's the wreck,' the skipper calls.

Ahead are some rusted steel plates jutting out of the water.

A mile further on the land swings sharply as we clear

the cape and head south into the protected waters of the gulf. We are into a big funnel of water that sweeps south for fifty miles before swinging up along the north-east coastline.

There is a gentle breeze. We stay on deck, quietly excited, watching the shore and the ocean. The skipper holds us on due south about a mile from the coast. Ernie is on the gunwale, chatting to the skipper through the wheelhouse window.

Charlie nudges me and says, 'There's the track.' A mile away, on the shore, is the bare strip over the low sandhills and the square brown gravel parking area near the beach.

We can't see the town but can picture it, away behind the hills with the track running through the low scrub towards the roofs shining in the late sun. And just beyond the beach and the line of sandhills is the cemetery. In half an hour we'll walk past it and I'll see the dried grass and row of gum trees, the red dirt and my father's grave.

The boat drops revs suddenly. I look up at the skipper in the wheelhouse. We are still a half a mile short of the anchorage. The skipper has only one hand on the wheel; he is leaning out of the window looking at something in the water.

A hundred yards away a large whale wallows in an oily swirl on the surface. All of its movements are slow. Part of the long smooth bulk arches over and rolls above the water and under again. Someone shouts. Sarge runs to the fo'c'sle to get his camera.

There seems to be no purpose to the whale's heavy, slow movements, but I think we all know it isn't playing. It is floundering.

Charlie stands up on the gunwale. 'What's wrong with it?'

'Don't know,' Sarge says. He is taking pictures.

'It's sick,' the skipper says. And then, still watching from the window, he pushes the throttle forward and the boat spreads a new wash of water to one side and we move on.

From the deck, looking back, we watch until there is only a glazed, oily strip of water.

I've heard stories about whales coming in to die. Why would they do it, I wonder. Why would they leave the deep water? I've read about people trying to hunt them out again. It must be strange for them to feel all of their crushing weight for the first time, rolling in the shallows. Never to be in deep water again.

Once I'd talked to an old man who had killed whales in the north-west in the early days when men rowed boats to chase them. And I'd seen the old, abandoned whaling station a hundred miles south of the cape with the broken ramps up the beach and old jetty posts near the shore and tanks, rusted boilers and white bones up higher on the low sandhills. I'd walked amongst the wreckage and there were turtle tracks from the shore leading to the shelter of mounds and little sandhills higher up.

When Claire was pregnant with Jane, Charlie had driven us out one night to watch the turtles lay their eggs. We went to the tip of the cape, below the lighthouse, and saw the rippled track across the beach, followed it in the moonlight to the bursts of sand spraying up and the turtle shovelling with her flippers as she dug the hole. She took no notice of the three of us crouching, watching.

We stayed there while the moon rose and the turtle dug

deeper and the little waves ripped along the shore like silk tearing. We saw her, big and slow moving, lay the eggs. Dozens of them, white, like ping-pong balls. And Charlie looked at Claire and said, 'Looks easy enough,' and she faked a swing at him with her hand, brought it back to brush the hair from her forehead, and smiled.

The boat is slowing down again. We are opposite the parking area on the beach and only four hundred yards offshore. I go down to the fo'c'sle. Charlie has his kitbag on the bunk. I lean through the hatch.

'Toss my bag up, will you, mate? Are you ready to go? He's nearly ready to drop the pick.'

'Be right with you.'

He tosses my bag up and climbs the little ladder out of the fo'c'sle. We are opposite the car park. Sarge tips the anchor over and the chain rattles out.

The sea is calm. Martin cuts the motor close to shore and the dinghy glides in and nudges the sand. We jump out and carry our kitbags up the beach and then pull the dinghy above the high-water mark. Martin trails the rope out and pushes the anchor down into the sand.

We walk up over the parking area and along the track that cuts through the sandhills.

The country is dry and we follow the track and pass the small cemetery. I don't go in or say anything as we walk.

'There's the old stockyards,' Charlie says.

Away on our right at the end of a narrow track are the rails and the windmill; this was the place we'd kept our horses. We'd ridden from here to the hills and the beach. I remember a night when we'd come back from a ride, watered the horses, gone to the pub in Charlie's ute and driven back to the beach. Claire came with us — it wasn't long after he'd met her. It was a hot moonlit night and she'd sat between us on the front seat. We'd pulled up at the parking area with the lights of the ute shining down across the beach to the ocean.

'It's so hot,' she'd said and peeled off her blouse.

We were all silent as she sat with her hair on her bare shoulders, her face and breasts pale in the moonlight as little creamy waves slapped along the shore.

In the west, behind the town, are the ranges. Hard dry scrub grows at the edge of the track, the spinifex and wattle powdered with red dust.

'Fuckin' dry,' the skipper says. 'Grow anything in this country if you could get water onto it.'

Ahead of us the iron roofs of the first houses shine silver. The houses start at the flat land on the western side of the track and spread up into the foothills of the ranges. Everything is still, but there is a buzz in the air from insects. The town, ahead of us, seems asleep in the sun.

We come to the transport company yard on the fringes of the town. A big red freezer truck is parked near a shed. The skipper goes in and we walk on along the road.

It is mid-afternoon when we reach the pub and very hot. Only a few cars are parked outside. We drop our kitbags in the beer garden on the patchy lawn and go into the bar. Two ceiling fans swish slowly. Four men sit along the bar on the high stools. The barmaid looks up as we come in.

She is pouring a beer and she glances away to look at us.

'Give us a jug,' Martin says. 'Hang on, make it two.'

She nods. 'Be right with you.'

We sit away from the bar at one of the tables. There are pictures of racehorses on the walls. It is cooler under one of the fans. We feel different, sitting there, waiting for the beer. Our hair is matted, faces burnt brown; we are fit and hardened from the work and feel proud, although it is never discussed.

The barmaid brings the beer and we all watch her lean down to put the jugs on the table.

Her arms are brown and she wears a short sleeveless green dress. She straightens up and wipes a hand quickly across her backside as if drying it and looks around, waiting to be paid. Martin hands her the money. She walks back behind the bar, chews the corner of her lip and flicks the till shut.

We feel the quietness, the stillness, in the cooler bar-room. It is different to be settled and sitting together after two weeks of rocking on the ocean. And we are all slightly off balance with this and with the barmaid's bare arms and the way she bends down and the green dress slides up her brown legs.

I glance over at her and she sees me and smiles. Her smile changes everything. It makes me realise that I've been thinking only of her smooth arms, her slightly moist lips; her smile makes me believe she wants me to know more about her, it lingers as if saying, 'Yes, it is what I want from you; I want you to see where my smile comes from.'

Martin has seen it too. 'Jesus Joey, she's keen, mate.'

I pick up my cigarettes and light one. Charlie seems distant. He is smoking too and I watch him scratch his leg and gulp down half a glass of beer, turn, look over his shoulder at the door. He is edgy, pulling hard on the cigarette. I know he's arranged for Claire to leave a message at the pub, and wonder why he hasn't asked.

'Skipper's taking his time,' Sarge says. 'Who's buying?'

'Give us it,' Martin says. He grabs the empty jug and is about to stand up when the barmaid walks over again.

'Another jug? You fellers are from the turtle boat, aren't you? Who's Charlie?'

He looks up at her.

'Claire's in town. She left a message for you. It's at the bar.'

Charlie follows her back to the bar. I see him asking questions while she fills the jug. He carries the beer back and sits down, leans over, tops up my glass and very quickly, probably not seen by the others, looks at me and raises his eyebrows. He knows she is in town now but doesn't seem to be completely relaxed.

The skipper walks in and sits down with us. 'Jesus. Got a glass? Bit fuckin' warm outside.' He goes to the bar, comes back with an empty glass, fills it and drinks the lot. He fills the glass again, wipes his mouth. 'I was talking to Mick, the truck driver. We unload at ten tomorrow morning. So we've all got to be ready to go first thing. Mick's given me his ute to run around in. I'm camping at his place tonight. He said there's a couple of spare beds if anyone else is interested.'

There is a crash behind the bar. The barmaid has dropped a glass. Someone whistles. There are a few more people in the bar now. She smiles, quickly. It is nothing, really. That's what her face seems to say.

Charlie nods his head towards the bar and says, 'Claire's staying with her.'

'Who? The barmaid?'

'Yeah. She got here a week ago. She's picked up a bit of casual work here. At the pub, I mean.'

'You going to get her?'

'Might go up in a while.'

'Where are they staying?'

'Top of the town. You'd know the house. We went there once to a party. Behind old Bruno's place.'

'Speak of the devil.'

Bruno is coming in the door. We both know him. He's lived in the town since the beginning. Our fathers had known him well. He is a solid and squat man about fifty years old of German descent. He has always been very friendly to me and, after my father died, I'd had a drink with him a few times. When he drinks too much he gets very serious but right now he is happy. He sees us. 'Ah ... you two. You teamed up with these other wild bastards, hey?' He comes over and shakes hands. 'But what you doing Joe? You see your mother yet? I see her yesterday, she know you coming with this boat. You better go to say hello.'

'Don't worry Bruno, I'll get there tonight.'

'Hey,' he leans down close to me. 'You can bring me fish, hey? Big one. Snapper. I pay you.'

'Yeah, we'll bring you some fillets. Next trip.'

'All right, good. Good.' And with a stiff wave of his arm he signals the end of the conversation and walks to the bar.

What he'd said makes me think of my mother. I'd have to go and see her soon. A couple more beers and I'd leave. But it is good to be with the crew. The bar is getting noisy. We know a few of the fellows who have come in. Everyone is loosening up. The skipper has started to tell his stories. 'We got a hundred and twenty once. In a day. That was in the old sixteen-foot dinghies. Big slow old bastards they were. Had to really work for your turtles then.'

'We still have to work for the buggers,' Martin says.

The skipper ignores him. 'Yeah, that was when Simpson was in charge,' he goes on. 'Mad bastard he was. If you didn't pull your weight he dumped you on the shore and that was it. He dumped blokes fifty miles south of the lighthouse. Try walking fifty miles out there. Jesus! Red hot.' He shakes his head, smiles, and drinks some beer.

'Dropped me at the beach one day to walk to the lighthouse for parts. Fuckin' miles away. Nearly killed me. Made it to an old tank, old windmill. Dry as a bone and full of bats!'

We wait for him to go on, but he only wipes his mouth with the back of his hand and seems sad, remembering.

'Yeah, give us another jug,' Martin says. The barmaid has come over to collect the empty jug.

'You going to go up and see Claire?' she asks Charlie.

He gives her a quick, challenging look.

'Can you get us that jug?' the skipper says. He passes the barmaid some money. 'Listen, if you fellers want a shower, want to get cleaned up, Mick says it's okay to use his place.' The barmaid walks away without smiling.

'What's going on tonight?' Ernie rolls a cigarette as he speaks.

'Bound to be something happening. This place comes to life a bit at night.'

'What about we have a shower and a feed and come back later on?'

'Cut it out, we just bloody got here.'

'Please yourself. I'm going up for a shower in a while.'

The barmaid carries the jug over. I clear a space for it and she puts it down. 'Thanks.'

She doesn't smile but her hand brushes the side of her forehead as she straightens up, as if following a movement she has forgotten that comes to her now as easily as the softness in her eyes that goes with it. But it flies from her quickly and I know she doesn't want the others to see it. Perhaps she doesn't even want me to see it. I'm not sure.

'What are you doing tonight, Joe?' Martin asks.

I know I will go to see my mother. But I am beginning to feel warmed and it is good to think of what might happen.

'If there's something going on down here later on — a band maybe — yeah, I'll be into it.'

Charlie picks up his beer and spills some of it. He is getting a bit drunk and looks like he is settling in, but he surprises me when he says to the skipper, 'Hey, can I take the ute for a while?'

'Yeah. You can drop me off, I'm going to Mick's for a shower and a spell, anyone else?'

'You coming mate?' Charlie asks me.

'Yeah, I'll come.'

I look over at the barmaid. She is working at the other end of the bar and doesn't see me.

We walk out, grab our kitbags and cross the car park to the ute. It has been in the sun and the seat is hot on our legs when we get in.

The skipper drives. The sun is low above the ranges in the west. I feel a bit hazy from the beer and heat. The streets are quiet, the houses seem closed up as if people are shut away from the glare of the outside world. Patches of lawn struggle in some of the yards but thin into yellow strands on the red dirt between the houses.

We are crammed into the front of the ute. Broken cobwebs of heat float in the distance above the black road. The skipper turns left and pulls up outside a house with a trailer parked near it.

'This is Mick's place,' he says. 'You fellers can take the ute but I'll need a lift back down the pub about seven.'

Charlie drives and we pass the hospital where Jane was born. He pulls up at a house and says, 'This is it.' His red Holden is in the yard and I can see Claire standing at a makeshift clothesline strung between the corner of the house and a tree in the back yard. She is draping a towel over the line and Jane is near her, sitting on the ground playing with some pegs. Jane hears the ute and stands up, watching, and Charlie gets out and she sees him and her face changes, comes alive and she turns, runs to her mum and grabs at her legs. Claire looks down and then over at us, smiles, scoops her daughter up and with her graceful, almost gentle walk, comes across the red dirt of the yard towards us.

She is browner than she'd been in the city and wears a white, loose, long-sleeved shirt with the sleeves rolled up. Her bare legs are long and brown. She puts Jane down. The little girl is shy. Charlie is shy, too. Perhaps he wants me to go. He puts his hand out and Jane takes it and he lifts her up. Claire says, 'You made it. We just came back from the beach. Hello, Joe.' She leans down, her face framed in the car window, touches my hand and says, 'Hi,' and then straightens up and puts her arm around

Charlie's shoulder, just gently, while he holds their daughter.

Charlie says to me, 'Thanks mate, you keep the ute. We'll see you down at the pub later on.'

I start the ute, back out onto the street and wave. They stand in a little group. Claire waves. Charlie is talking to Jane and playfully messing up her hair.

I decide not to go straight to my mother's place and drive to a gravel track that runs past the last houses and up into the foothills of the ranges and I follow it until I am nearly at the two big tanks. These tanks are part of the water supply for the houses. I stop the ute and get out and sit on the bonnet, the town spread out below me. The sun is behind my back, low over the ranges, perhaps an hour away from setting. Beyond the town the ocean in the gulf is flat and pale blue. There is no movement and from where I sit it seems distant and lifeless. I can see the small dark shape of the turtle boat anchored out off the beach. In the south the sweep of ocean and land is blurred in a silvery haze. To the east it is clearer. The islands are smudges on the north-west horizon. Between me and the sea are the quiet, shining, roofs of the houses. They are silver against the red land and beyond them the road begins its two-hundred mile path to the next town south. I can see the little track branching off to the stockyards and the cemetery and then all of the flat country to the north with the broken, darker lines of dried creek beds and I can picture the way we rode our horses across that country and it seems longer than two, maybe three, years ago.

I am half drunk, but the softening of the sky as the sun drops settles into me. I get off the bonnet and in behind the wheel, start the motor and head back down to the town and my mother's place.

She is just coming out of the house and down the steps as I pull up and she sees me and claps her hands together in the old-fashioned way that a child praying at the bedside would; it is one clap together as if one is enough for everything. She is very happy to see me and walks quickly over, saying, 'Well, the traveller returns.'

We go into the house and she makes a cup of tea. My mother is burnt brown from the sun and moves quickly around the little kitchen, getting the cups out, pouring the hot water in, talking, organising. 'You'll be hungry. Here, have a bit of this' — taking out bread, spreading honey on it — 'Now, you'll be here for a few days? Don't let me forget … there are some of your old shorts and shirts, I put some away the other day — you might need them out there — you may as well take them. What about hats?'

I ask about my father's grave. I want to know what it is for her now.

'Oh! You should see! The Sturt's peas are in bloom. Beautiful they are. Absolutely beautiful. Come on. Come out and have a look, only take five minutes, and I have to water them anyway.'

We finish the tea. She is moving around again, filling a water bottle at the sink and then, quickly, we are out the door, in the ute, on our way.

I stop at the cemetery gate. The sun has just gone behind the ranges and there is a soft light on the graves as we walk in towards them past the row of gum trees with their pale trunks.

I see the blood red flowers on my father's grave. My

mother bends down, scoops a little ring of dry dirt from around the stems and empties the water bottle onto the earth.

I stand still; surprised, even shocked, to see the place again. Here under this red dirt is my father. Here, where each wild flower burns like a little red flame.

It is peaceful walking back to the car in the quietness of the dying light and there is a rich stillness in the air and in my heart. The pale trunks of the gum trees in the dusk have turned a dull pink and the leaves above gently stir. They are like naked girls who discover that their blushing colour is coming out of the earth and begin to move freely with it in a dance.

FOUR

The trees that line the path to my father's grave, with their silky smooth trunks, are very different from the one I can see now through the window: it is old, so old, with thick branches and grey, twisted bark.

Sonny likes to climb. Some days you'll see him on it, quite high, legs casually hanging, a bright little smile and calling, 'Dad. Hey Dad!'

We had some people out here last night. Sally had said a few days ago that she wanted her friend Miriam to come for dinner so I asked a couple of my old friends too. The weather looked good so we decided to make it a barbecue. It was a bit unusual really, we don't socialise much.

An hour or so before they arrived I was sitting down, doing some writing, working on this story and Sally said, 'Do you want to give the toilet a clean?'

'Do I want to?'

'You know what I mean.'

'Why don't you just say, "Will you clean the toilet?"'

'Don't worry about it.'

She was making salads. I saw Sonny look up. He hates

fights and has some kind of built-in sensor which registers a fight building long before the first angry word has been shouted. When I looked at him he said, 'You said you wouldn't yell anymore, Dad.'

I went down to clean the toilet and was in there when he walked past the door and looked in, sizing up any changes in my mood. I said, 'Don't worry, I'm not going to get wild.' He seemed satisfied and didn't cry, which he sometimes will do: he was all right, after a while I saw him outside playing with the dog.

I got over it too and lit the barbecue and Sally came out to the verandah and started setting everything up. She was making it all nice: putting a cloth over the outside table; she swept the floorboards, walked over to the jacaranda tree and picked some of the soft mauve flowers and put them into a little vase.

'Now, what do you think? That's all right isn't it?' She stood back, looking at the flower arrangement.

I reached over and adjusted a little sprig of flowers. They looked pretty.

'Do you want to do some onions now, before they get here? Then I can keep them warm in the oven.'

'Yeah, okay.'

I went inside and got a beer and the onions and came out and cut them up on a jarrah breadboard, tossed them on the hotplate and sat back, looking down the valley at the way the last of the sunlight shone over the gum trees on the ridge.

Sonny came around the side of the house. The dog was running near the fence, shaking the old shoe in her jaws.

Sonny saw me standing at the barbecue, turning the onions.

'Can I do that Dad?'

'You can do absolutely anything you like. Do you know why?'

'Why?'

''Cos you're a special feller, that's why.'

'Dad, I told you not to say silly stuff.'

He took the long fork and stood at the barbecue, reaching over, stabbing at the onions.

He had it under control; he's pretty handy at doing things and, once he's mastered something, hates anyone to help. He could change the wheels on his skateboard just after he turned five. He'd find the right size ring spanner, sit cross-legged on the verandah and unscrew the nuts, swap the wheels around and then tighten the nuts again; the whole job might take him half an hour. There are other times though, if something is broken and he can't manage, that he loves a bit of help and will quietly sit and watch while I work on it.

Not long ago I fixed a broken toy gun for him and then we went out for a walk in the paddock while he waved the thing around and took deliberate aim at imaginary enemies. The old horse wandered over and I hoisted Sonny up and led him around for a while until he fired off a couple of loud clicks at something, probably a low flying spaceship, and the horse reared up and Sonny fell down to the ground.

It's amazing how something like that can change a little kid. He's wary of the horse now. I hope it won't last but it probably will.

He was reaching over, poking at the onions.

'Listen to that,' I said, 'Can you hear it? What is it?'

He didn't look up. There was a sharp 'pipe pipe pipe'

sound from a tree out near the fence. I walked over and looked up and could see two twenty-eight parrots on a branch. It was a new kind of sound, I hadn't heard it before.

'Is Sonny out there?' Sally called from the kitchen. 'Tell him to come in and take some of this stuff out for me.'

I walked inside. She was grating a carrot at the bench with her back to me. I put my hands on her shoulders. 'Are you doing your special preparation thing?'

'Have you decided to get friendly?'

'I'm always friendly.'

She tucked a shoulder up near her ear and said, 'I've got to get this done.' She turned to me, raised her eyebrows and half smiled. It was her old cheeky look and it made me feel good that she wasn't cranky.

When I walked out to the verandah carrying a bowl and some glasses, the dog had dropped the shoe and was standing still, looking up the driveway. I went around the side of the house. A car had pulled up. It was Tony. He had Chris with him.

At about nine o'clock I took the little bloke in to his bed. The rest of them were out on the verandah. I could hear their talk and laughter.

I sat on the bed near Sonny.

'Story?' he asked.

'Just a quick one.'

'What story?'

'Well, let's see. Do you want me to read or just tell one?'

'Read.'

'Okay.'

I started looking around for one of his books and then went over to the bed, leaned down, kissed him and said,

'Listen, we'll have a story tomorrow night. Okay? You just go to sleep now.'

He looked right into me and said, 'All right.'

'Goodnight, little jumbuck.'

'Goodnight, Dad.'

I got up and he watched with his golden hair on his forehead, his eyes trying to hold me back. The room was a mess. His clothes were all over the floor. He gets that from me. I turned the light off.

'Dad?'

'Yeah.'

'Can you leave the door open a bit?'

'Okay. Goodnight.'

I went back out to the verandah. Everyone had pushed back a bit, settling in. Sally was talking to Miriam. She's single now, about forty, has a couple of teenage kids, dresses well, throws her head back when she laughs, laughs a lot, attacks conversations concerning her work with real intensity.

'No, no, no,' she said. 'Sally, I don't think you can ... I don't think you can just let people like that set up programs that are in direct conflict with ours.'

Sally was ready. 'No, of course you can't but you have to have an alternative: you have to be able to show that their ideas are totally hopeless and that yours are supporting an industry.'

Miriam wiped her lip, held her wine glass. 'Absolutely, but you know, what really peeves me is that it's government money, taxpayers' money, being used, with the sole intention of trying to run private operations out of business.'

'It's not just that,' Sally began, but she saw me watching her and hesitated.

I went over and sat down near Chris and Tony. They're both old friends.

The moon had risen, white and high, out above the paddocks. Sally had turned to Miriam again and was making another point. I wasn't really listening.

'How's your drink?' I asked.

Tony shook his head. Chris was rolling a cigarette. He looked up. 'No, no — I'm right thanks.'

I picked up my beer can and gulped what was left in it, went back inside to the fridge, took another one and walked out again.

'So,' I said to Chris, 'what do you think?'

He licked his cigarette paper, screwed up his eyes, gave me his quizzical look and said, 'About what?'

I laughed. It was what I expected: you put an obscure question to Chris and he'll give you back his slightly affronted, challenging look, giving the impression that anything you can toss at him he'll be ready for.

Tony studied the wine in his glass, twirled it gently.

'What about you?' I said to him, 'Not going to sleep over there, are you?'

He was listening to Sally and Miriam talking and I could tell he was waiting to enter into it; he glanced up quickly but more or less ignored me.

It made me happy, knowing that he would. Because you're ready for it Tony, aren't you? You understand these moments and you know that I like you to see me turn against myself; you know that I want you to beat off these little attacks because that's the arrangement we've always been happy with; that is how we've known our place with each other. And it's no different now, even now: I can't let you dig deep into my kitbag to see what's buried there and I can't let you want to do it.

Tony glanced at me again and I laughed. He didn't know why and nor did I, really. I only knew it was good to be with friends; it made me feel reckless and happy.

'You want a beer?' Chris asked me.

'All right.'

He went inside and came out and sat down again, opened his beer and said, 'What's all this about you going off to do some teaching?'

'That's the plan.'

'So ... where would you go? You mean teach locally or you'd let them send you off somewhere?'

'Yeah. Go anywhere. I need some work.'

'Well, that's a big move ... still, you've done it before.'

Yes, I had, but not for a long time. I'd done some teaching a few years after I'd finished the fishing. Sally had taught too. We'd spent a year in the north at an Aboriginal school and after that, a year down here. And that was it. Short and sweet.

'Are you going off teaching, Joe?' It was Miriam, interrupting her own conversation with Sally to cut in.

'Well, I don't know yet. Maybe. If they give me some work.'

'And what do you think about that?' she asked, turning to Sally.

'Can't wait to get rid of him,' Sally said, laughing. 'I think he'd go very well in a one-horse town out in the bush.'

We all laughed.

Tony said, 'Listen Joe, you've done this Aboriginal teaching thing, now, what do you think about it all?'

'What?'

'The Aboriginal problem, where do you sit on it?'

I used to be shy about my opinions when I was younger, or maybe I just didn't know where I stood on a lot of issues. I'm not really political and even those things I was passionate about, well ... I'm not sure any more. There's sometimes a dark wave that moves in me, a dark doubt, but there are times when I know, instinctively, how to beat it: I have to hook into something that really moves me and it's like hooking into a big fish, I never know if I'll land it and that's probably why I said, 'I was with a group of Aboriginal kids once, sitting in the dirt under a boab tree. We'd come out of the classroom, it was hot, so we went out there for a while to sit and tell stories, they love doing that. Anyway, I noticed they were really interested, really listening and their hands seemed to float; they became so much a part of the story that their bodies seemed to flow into what was around them. We were sitting there, one of them was telling the story and the others ... well, their hands were making these little patterns in the dirt, just this gentle stroking and touching of the earth. I was next to a girl; we were all in a circle and I watched her hands moving in the dirt as she listened and her hands were so black alongside mine and a couple of times as she made these slow swirls her hand touched mine but she didn't notice. It's almost like they become the earth, they are the earth; growing in it and out of it and into the story.'

Sally picked up the wine and poured herself half a glass. 'Some more?' She held the bottle towards Miriam.

'Just a drop.'

'Listen Joe,' Chris said, 'I understand what you're saying but, I mean, life goes on doesn't it? You can't ignore change. You can't live in the past. Any number of things can change the direction of a culture. They were here, sure, but things change, you can't put the blame for what happened two hundred years ago on today's generation. What are we supposed to do? Say we're sorry, for Christ's sake? What good is that going to do?'

'Yeah,' Sally said. 'You can't change anything now; everyone has to have the same treatment now, white, black, whoever ...'

Tony shifted in his seat, leaned forward. 'Well, you know, people might just be ready for a change of heart.'

'No, I don't think so, Tony,' Sally cut in. 'People don't just have changes of heart: you mean they're going to spend all their lives having nothing to do with these people, basically not giving a stuff about them and all of a sudden: click! They're just going to change? Don't think so.'

'Well, yeah, why not?' Tony said.

'Look,' I said, 'I don't think it's all about a change of heart, I think it's more to do with people discovering what's actually in their hearts, having a bit of a look and finding what it is that they've buried in there.'

'And what's that going to do?' Sally asked.

'Yes, that's right, what can it do?' Chris added.

'People have to know what they believe in,' I said, 'and that sometimes takes a while to work out, but if you do work it out I suppose you're in a better position to do something about the problem.'

'People know what they believe in,' Sally said. 'Most of them just believe in getting on with their lives, there's no big mystery for them about what they believe in.'

'But if they're just getting on with their lives,' I

answered, 'they're probably not taking too much notice of anyone else's life.'

'Listen,' she said. 'Why should they? If everyone took responsibility for themselves, was responsible for their own happiness and welfare, well, we wouldn't have half of these problems.'

'That's just a batten down the hatches attitude,' I answered. 'You finish up with a society where people run into their house, lock all the doors, peep out from behind the bloody curtain. No trust. Stranger danger! What bullshit. Going into the schools. Teaching little kids that every poor bloke on the street is some kind of potential axe murderer. Houses look like bloody prisons. Steel grates. Spotlights.'

'Joe! Ssshhh! That's all bulldust. It's just life. Just get on with it. You can't afford to be worrying about everyone else, you have to get on with your own life.'

'But we don't live on our own, do we? We're not alone at all.'

'You'll be on your own if you try to solve the world's problems and forget about your own.'

It was just Sally and me, now. The others were quiet. I wanted to really get at something: pull out a hard chunk of truth and throw it on the table to dazzle. But I was uneasy that the focus had shifted onto the two of us and the last thing I wanted was for Sally and me to be wriggling under the microscope. I looked over at her and knew that she was really ready, and that settled it.

'Oh well,' I said, 'You're probably right, we don't seem to sort out these things by arguing about them anyway, let's drop it.'

The moon was beautiful and clear and high but I was

the only one looking at it and the shine seemed to have gone off the night.

Sally made coffee and we chatted for another half hour, but it wound down quickly and by eleven they'd all gone.

'Do you want another coffee?' Sally asked. She'd started to clear up the table.

'No. No, I'm right, thanks.'

She carried on with the bowls, the plates, bottles and cans and after a while I heard the kettle boil in the kitchen and the clink of a cup and she came out and said, 'Goodnight,' and went into the house and everything was quiet again except, once or twice, I heard the lonely, distant sound of a mopoke over near the ridge.

Chris had left his lighter on the table. It was silver and old-fashioned. I flicked the little wheel. A flame jumped up. I turned off the verandah light and sat in the cool moonlight. A patchwork of blurred shadow from the lattice fell across my legs and the table. I flicked the lighter a few more times. The house was quiet now. I wanted to go in and get Lizzie's diary from our bedroom but wasn't sure if Sally was asleep.

I smoked a cigarette and then went in and opened the drawer quietly in the dark. I couldn't hear Sally breathing, which made me think she might be awake. I stepped softly from the room and took the diary out to the verandah, switched the light on again and sat down.

January 11, 1886. Harry started to the Margaret River with thirteen head of cattle. Mr Armstrong was missing this morning. Has been very unwell during the day and last night.

January 12. Mr A better today and I finished the needlework. Baked — very busy — cleaned up. I rode Boland and Mr A Whalebone — took Smiler for Robey and off we went. Mr A and I went to Browns and made oath as required. I lost one half of my name, it appears I was christened Eliza instead of Elizabeth as I always thought but no matter I suppose.

January 13. Memorable day for us, I changed my name altogether and am now Eliza Armstrong.

Had it very quiet, only a few at the church door to pelt us with rice and flowers. Had a good dinner of the cake, it weighed 15 lb. I wrote a letter to Father, left a good lump of cake for him and we carried about 5 lb home also some rum and some wine.

Jan 15. Minnie brought us news. It appears such a scandalous affair was never heard of before as our wedding.

Jan 18. Harry came riding Lucifer with a letter from Father returning my 3 last letters with a message on the back of the last one that he desired our correspondence to cease, does not intend to speak to me again.

Jan 19. Mailboy heard Father at the bridge this morning going on dreadful about us — we cannot comfort each other much, but it is no fault of ours.

I wondered if she'd sat, sadly. I wanted to see behind the sentences of her life. It was easy to dream of what I didn't know; her face, her eyes, her dreams. There seemed a rhythm in her that came not from her words but from how she must have brought herself to the table to write. It was sad reading about the birth of her first child, knowing she'd died with the last. And what would she have written if she could? 'I'm feeling poorly. Doctor not coming. Mr Armstrong away with cattle.' Probably. She'd have kept it simple like the first:

Nov 24 1886. I took ill in the night and am very bad. Things in a pretty fix. However Harry made a start with the cattle and a note to Mother. Minnie rode Smiler and took a note for Mrs Henty. She came in time to see my baby born at 3 o'clock in the evening — a little girl, alas.

Nov 25. Poor Mr Armstrong quite behind in his work today. Mrs Henty and everybody else very busy. Am very well indeed but not able to work yet.

But what happened with your last child Lizzie, your fifth?

Maybe your husband had to ride off to hunt cattle for a couple of days and you saw him disappear into the thicket of scrub below the karri trees and stood at the rail and then walked over to sit on a slab of granite above the creek. And walking slowly, heavily, back to the house the pain leapt into you. Did you lean against the door and pray that someone might come, that perhaps Billy, the Aboriginal boy would be passing taking cattle to the swamp block? Later, lying on the bed, your hands resting lightly on your tight stomach, I see you looking out through the small window at the pale, cold light of the night. Holding, holding. Listening to the magpies before dawn. Hearing the cattle. Going to the door to see Billy riding behind them, his face smiling but changing when he sees how your hands clutch low at the full weight. Wheeling his horse at your words: 'Bring Mrs Henty, Billy. Bring her fast.'

Did you see the dark woman, Patsy, bend to the fire and the steaming pot of water and hear Mrs Henty's voice saying, 'I'll just sponge you down, there now, there now, my love. Patsy, bring more water.'?

Heaving, heaving. The clenched face of Mrs Henty and her hands bloody. Wiping them on her heavy apron. A smear of blood on her chin. The timber walls close, unyielding. The lantern flickering and, for a moment, Mrs Henty's hands flying into giant shadows on the walls, flying like trapped crows around the dim room, coming together to beat and tear at the side of her face.

And goodbye Lizzie, goodbye, while Patsy holds the bloodied child and Mrs Henty bends down, strokes the damp strands of hair from your forehead and whispers, 'Sure, it was God's way. Sure, you're a brave soul and it was just God's way, just God's way.'

When I went into the bedroom Sally was asleep, or she seemed asleep and the moonlight came through the big window and I could see her hair against the sheet. I got into the bed and lay on my back for a long time until I heard the steady rhythm of her breathing and then I reached out and touched her bare arm for a moment, but nothing changed and I stayed just the way I was, looking out of the window and feeling the same.

In the morning I woke early, an hour before the sun, and could hear the magpies. They were making smooth rolling calls, so different from the harsh attacking cries when they have young birds in the nest and sit watching, waiting, whacking their beaks on the branch.

I walked into the kitchen and then outside the house. It was a calm, cool morning but I knew it would get hot; there was just a hint of a light north-easterly breeze.

I had no plans, but I walked over to the big peppermint tree, saw the long bamboo pole leaning against it and decided to go fishing. There was no bait. The little canvas fishing bag was hanging over a branch, it had nothing in it either, no hooks or sinkers. I went back into the house. Sonny was up, he must have heard me. He stood in the kitchen, rubbing his eyes, looking groggy.

'Have some breakfast, mate.'

'What?'

'Might go fishing.'

I went out and put the old flick rod on the ute and walked back to the house for a knife.

'You right, Sonny? I'll get you a hat.'

Going out along the driveway I said to him, 'Are you awake, little feller? Are you ready to catch about four thousand and twenty-nine herring?'

It was just over a kilometre to the beach. There were a couple of cars heading down; early morning surfers, but the road was fairly quiet. We came around the last bend before climbing the slow sweep of hill, passed the sharp drop down to the river and then to the edge of the ridge. The horizon, soft sky, blue, still ocean, was suddenly all below and ahead of us and we went down into it on the black road.

I turned onto a side track, drove along it for a hundred metres and we stopped, and below us was the beach and the ocean.

It all looked too calm and perfect for herring, but there was a bank of weed on the beach that was old, maybe a week old, anyway. We got out and I untied the rod and gave one end to Sonny, grabbed the canvas bag and down we went, down the last bit of hill, Sonny behind, holding his end of the rod like a sleepy little boy who's just realised the importance of the mission.

When we came to the weed bank a wave washed up near it and I said, 'That's good, there's a bit of swell; herring don't like it too calm. Right, now we have to look for maggots.'

I pulled some of the weed out of the pile and saw maggots underneath.

'Oh, there's heaps, Dad! There's heaps of maggots,' Sonny said.

I tossed a couple of bunches of weed at the edge of the water and then threaded about six maggots onto the hook and pushed the rod in the sand. It stuck up high out of the beach.

We watched for a little while and didn't see any fish bubbling near the shore. I walked to the water with the rod and flicked the line out. I dragged back and flicked it behind me and then saw a little island of bubbles and slashes on the surface.

'There they are.'

I flicked out again into the broken water, dragged back and the rod tip bent over and I whipped it up and a little silver herring sailed over my head and landed on the beach. Sonny squatted down next to it.

'You want to get it off the hook?'

'No, you do it, Dad.'

We dug a hole in the sand and I dropped the herring in. Sonny squatted near the hole watching the herring twitch around.

I walked down, tossed out. Another one hit straight away. I called Sonny. He came running. The water washed up around his knees and he held the long rod with me and we swayed it back and the fish flew over our heads.

I fished for half an hour. Sonny played on the sand near the fish. Sometimes he'd run down, shouting, 'Dad, we've got eleven herring now,' and 'Dad, we've got twelve of them.'

After another ten minutes I'd caught a couple more. We had enough. I looked around for Sonny. He wasn't on the beach. I looked along it, both ways, and couldn't see him. I dropped the rod and ran to the narrow track that came down out of the sandhill. I shouted out and then saw him sitting on a bare patch behind some scrubby bushes drawing in the dirt with a stick.

'What?' He looked at me.

'No, nothing, it's all right, I just didn't know where you were. Come on, come and pack up the herring.'

He didn't say anything but I could tell from his eyes that he was wondering about what he saw in my face.

On the track that winds back into the house Sonny wanted to steer, so I pulled him onto my knee and he swung the wheel left and right, mucking around, running us off the track and back onto it, laughing. He hunched over the wheel, hands gripping it tightly, and tugged it around.

'Faster, Dad!'

I cleaned the herring and tossed the roe into a hot frying pan and Sonny and I ate them on buttered toast. They were shrivelled and crunchy.

When Sally came out she said, 'You got a few fish, that's good,' and walked through to the verandah.

I made coffee, took it out and sat with her at the little table in the sunlight.

'Do you want a herring?'

She shook her head. 'No thanks.'

There were a couple of kangaroos in the valley, mooching quietly around, eating the grass, bending and rising and then I saw another one lying down and something about its easy restful shape reminded me of schoolgirls when they sprawl on the lawn to eat their lunch and chat.

A kangaroo stood up, rock still, and looked across the paddock as if someone had called out, 'Hey! What the hell do you think you're doing?' and then swivelled its head towards the bush where another voice might have shouted, 'That's right, we mean you, buddy! What's the big idea?'

I've reached a point in the story where, having no clear view of the landscape ahead, I must walk quietly and slowly. The only things that are clear are certain motives I have: I want Sally to hold me and love me and I want to do the same to her; I want to tell jokes again and sing songs; I want to have control of my thoughts; I want to step out of my old clothes and into some new ones (a well-dressed chap with a swagger!); I want to be as truthful as a dead herring on a plate. I want to grab a harpoon and kill this thing I'm hunting.

'Are you there, Charlie?' No answer. His car has gone. I walk back to the ute and start it and the lights pick out

Claire's towel and bathers hanging on the clothesline.

I drive to the truckie's house. The skipper is sitting out on the step drinking a can of beer. He walks over and gets in.

He seems completely different to just a few hours earlier: shaved, scrubbed-looking; his mood is lively and tough, he's put on clean, fresh clothes, his hair is wet and combed. He's still in charge; no boat now, rolling under his legs, but I have the feeling that he is probably already thinking about a few of his favourite stories.

I drive past a group of young people walking along the street towards the pub. We can hear their laughter. They are bustling along, excited. At the edge of the group one girl is almost skipping, trying to keep up.

When we walk across to the pub the skipper says, 'There they are.' They are all out in the beer garden. Wooden tables and chairs have been pushed together. I see Jane, away from the main group, near a tree. A cat sits on a low branch and she is standing, watching it. There is a bigger crowd in the bar now.

Martin comes out of the door holding a full jug of beer and a glass. He sees me and shouts, 'Hey! Joey! Here! C'm'ere!' He has a cigar in his mouth. 'Here mate, get a beer into you, we're over here.' He waves with the jug, slopping some of the beer out.

We walk over to the table. The skipper says, 'You fellers had a feed yet Martin?'

'Hey?' Martin says. 'Tucker? Nah, too busy drinking.' He puts the jug down on the table. Charlie stands up. 'Here, grab a seat.'

'See your mum?' Claire asks. She's holding a glass of wine and wearing a skirt and a check blouse and her hair has been brushed wet and is smooth against her neck.

'Yes, she's good.'

I look down and her legs are stretched out near mine. She has sandals on.

'We're going to get some tucker,' Charlie says, 'You hungry? Want a steak sandwich? Have something to eat, hey? There's a band on in the other bar later on.'

'Ruth's knocking off at nine,' Claire says. 'She's going to mind Jane.'

'That's the barmaid,' Charlie says. 'What's the time now?'

'About eight.'

I look past the table and the beer garden and catch a glimpse of her in behind the bar and the crowd.

The skipper walks out with some empty glasses. Martin puffs on his cigar, nods at the jug and says, 'Fill 'em up out of that. Hey Joe, you coming in to the band later? Liven 'em up a bit?' He holds his glass towards the skipper. 'Yeah, top her up — good band, they reckon.'

He sucks on the cigar again, draws the smoke right in, blows it out.

'Set 'em alight, hey?' I say. 'Yeah, I'll have a look.' I turn to Claire. Jane is sitting on her knee now, sipping the squash. 'So, what's it like? Living up here, I mean, working at the pub. Do you like it?'

She reaches down and helps Jane settle the glass on the table. 'It's worked out so well, I was just lucky, and Ruth is good. You'll meet her, she's coming out later, but we've got heaps of room and I only have to work four shifts a week and that's enough and we've got Charlie's car so I can take Jane to the beach and she loves it down there. Yeah, it's really good.'

'Hey fellers! Have one of these!' Martin pulls a packet of cigars out of his pocket.

'Here, grab one.'

He passes them around.

Sarge says, 'Wouldn't smoke one of those if you paid me.'

'Listen, you fellers,' the skipper taps his cigar on the table, grips it in his teeth and strikes a match. 'Listen, now have a few tonight.' He lights the cigar. 'Have a few drinks, make a bit of a night of it — that's fair enough — but we unload in the morning and that means everyone. There's no favours, everyone at the beach at eight o'clock.' He draws on the cigar, picks up his beer glass. 'In the meantime, of course, make the most of it, gentlemen.' He raises his glass and smiles.

Claire is watching Charlie. 'Look how brown you all are,' she says, touching Charlie's arm. 'Look,' she strokes his skin, 'you just get brown so fast in the sun up here. Look at me. And this is only after two weeks.'

She stretches her legs carelessly out in front of her, pulls her skirt higher above her knees.

'Not as dark as you though,' she says to Charlie. 'You're like an Aboriginal,' and she flicks the skirt down again with the back of her hands.

'They used to live here once,' I tell her.

'Who? Aboriginals? Really?'

'Yeah … there are a few stories about why they left and won't come back. Some people say it's a sacred burial ground around here. Others reckon there was a huge tidal wave years ago.'

Charlie says nothing. Claire's right. He is a bit like an Aborigine. Moves like one. He stands with the harpoon on his shoulder, his hair ropey, and turns to signal and flows without effort. And he sees well, too. Deep into the water. Not as well as they would, of course. But he can see a shadow go across the sunlight under the surface.

My father had an Aboriginal friend when he was young, a boy who lived with his family across the valley, and I'd heard stories about the two of them riding to the river where they'd stand on the high rock, throw a piece of soap out into the dark water and then dive to find it. They'd tie the horses to the paperbark trees and play and swim until it was time to ride back across the hills. My father had told me how, years later, he'd gone to the hospital to see his old friend, but the face was tired, the eyes dull and he wouldn't speak.

'What happened to him?' I'd asked.

'He died in the end. Pointed the bone at himself, that's what he did.'

I suppose I always knew that it wasn't something that had actually happened, just my father's way of saying that his friend had been broken. Or maybe my father meant something else. I never really knew.

Martin passes the jug around and empties it. I reach out to take it from him.

'I'll get another one.'

'No. Bullshit.' He gets up and heads towards the bar. I follow him. When we go through the door the noise of talk and laughter hits us like a wave and we are caught in it and swimming against it. I see Bruno halfway along the bar talking in his serious way to a man who has his head down looking at his beer.

Martin pushes forward. He elbows his way through

and knocks against a big man in a blue singlet standing at the bar. The big bloke turns and says, 'Hey, what are you fuckin' doing?'

Martin puts the empty jug on the bar. He doesn't say anything or take his eyes off the face above the blue singlet.

'You young pricks think you can come into town and take over the joint. Now fuck off.' He shoves Martin in the chest but doesn't connect solidly and his big, hairy arms are still reaching out when his head seems to twist and tuck down into his shoulder. There is blood on his lip and he rocks and reaches for his mouth. Martin rips another punch into his belly. The big fellow steps back. I know it is over. You can see the uncertainty in his eyes.

I grab Martin. 'Leave him, come on.'

He is tense. His fists are clenched.

'Martin! Come on! Look at him. It's finished.'

He looks at me quickly, his eyes alight. 'Better get that jug then,' he says and turns to look hard at the man he's hit as if there is still something one of them might say.

I buy a jug and hand it to him. 'Here, take this out, I'll be there in a minute.' Bruno has caught my eye from along the bar.

'Yeah, righto, you coming out?'

'Be right there.'

He smiles and walks out with the jug of beer.

The big fellow is leaning on the bar as if there is nowhere else to be. I walk towards Bruno. Some of the drinkers are talking about it.

'He's fast, the young bloke.'

'Nah, not that fast. Big Bob's as slow as a fuckin' wet week. End of story.'

'Bruno. How are you?'

He puts out his burly arm guiding me to the bar and then grabs me around the shoulders and hugs me. There are two fresh beers on the bar.

'For you,' he says, pointing. 'Joe, what you do? What for all this fighting?'

'Don't know, Bruno.'

He looks heavy, serious.

'You know,' his face comes close to mine, 'I come to this country, what for? Your father, he was good man.' He pauses, his heavy eyes locked into something he must have seen in mine. 'Good man. Good. And he is in the war and I am on the other side, what you think? But, before he, you know, always before he dies we can talk, yes, always. Good friend.' He drinks some beer. 'What do you think is life, Joe? For fight?'

'I don't know, Bruno.'

He looks at me sadly and shakes his head. It is good to talk to him but I want to get back to the others. He asks about my mother and I tell him how we went to the cemetery. It seems to make him happier. I finish my beer and catch the barmaid's eye. She walks over.

'I have to go Bruno. I'll buy you one.'

'No. No.'

'Yes.'

'Hello,' the barmaid says. 'Are you going outside? I'm coming out soon. I knock off at nine. Two beers?'

'Thanks.'

She pours the beers, 'Has your mad mate settled down? Bob had it coming anyway.'

I shake hands with Bruno. He holds my hand for a long time.

'See you, Bruno.'

I pick up my beer and walk outside. The skipper is talking. He stops, waiting for me to sit down.

'Joe, I was just telling this lot … look, the thing is, if some crazy bastard wants to be a hero, well, okay, you gotta look after yourself, but what I'm saying is, we've got to do business in this town … unload the bloody boat, buy tucker, buy fuel, buy beer … okay? You got the message? Just think about it.' He stands up. 'I'm going inside, going to have a beer with Mick … think about it, okay?'

When he walks away, Martin becomes the centre of our thoughts. He seems to be twitching with pride; his eyes are bright and move quickly from me to Charlie, Claire, Ernie, all around.

Claire is the first to speak. 'Jane, here, come on.'

She holds out her hand and Jane looks up; she's been playing on the ground. Claire cuddles her and drops her chin onto the little girl's head and hugs tightly, rocking. 'Ruth is coming soon, she's going to look after you.' She rocks and talks softly and Jane is quiet now and sleepy.

Martin is glowing and it seems to me, for a little while, in the silence, we are all in his shadow.

'Here she comes,' Claire says. Ruth walks across the worn dry grass of the beer garden towards us. She flicks a little wave of hair from her forehead with a brisk movement of her hand. 'Wow. I'm glad that's over,' she says, and, looking at Jane, 'Oh, is she asleep already?' Jane is curled in her mother's arms. 'I can take her home now.'

'She's all right for a minute.' Claire strokes Jane's hair. 'Sit down for a while, have a break.'

'Hey Joe!' Martin says, 'What's happening? We going to

have a look at this band or what?'

Groups of people are walking along the path at the side of the pub and going in through the door to the main bar.

'Yeah. Let's get in there,' Charlie says.

'Are you going in?' Ruth asks me. She brushes her hair back again as she speaks. She has sat down right next to me and there is a shine on her face and neck.

Martin looks at me. 'What are you doing Joe?'

I don't answer.

He stands up. 'All right, you lot sort yourselves out, I'm off.' He walks away and calls back at us, 'See you in there.'

'What are you going to do?' I ask Ruth. 'Do you want a hand with Jane? Are you taking Charlie's car?' I feel drunk and my questions sound stupid but I want to be with her.

She smiles and I feel as if a cold wind has blown into me. In that moment I know nothing but hope, and no way to be sure. I have no clear thoughts, only the coldness inside and rising on my legs.

'Yes, okay then, if you could drive us home, that would be good.'

I get up quickly before anything changes. Charlie seems unsure, but when I say, 'I'll go and find the skipper to get the ute keys,' he gets up.

'No,' he says, 'just take my car. Bring it back later.'

He takes Jane from Claire and hoists her up so her head rests sleepily against him. Claire picks up a leather bag from the table, slings the thin strap over her shoulder and says, 'Yes, take the car, we'll be all right.'

Charlie silently passes Jane to me. I start walking

towards his car with Ruth and call back over my shoulder, 'I'll be back later.'

'Just lay her down on the back seat,' Ruth says.

I start the car and swing out of the parking area onto the road, and the dark lines and lights of the pub, the shape of shadows, the full outline of the tree in the beer garden and the bright windows of the bar all roll away from us with the black road ahead and Ruth beside me.

'Is your friend always like that?' she asks, and her voice jumps into me from the close, black silence. I change gears, not knowing what she means.

'Who?'

'What's his name? Martin. The fighter.'

'Oh … yes, he's a little bit crazy. Sometimes you don't know what he's going to do.'

'He's younger than you, isn't he?'

'Couple of years younger, about nineteen I think. He's all right, he's a good worker.'

'Turn right here, right!'

I swing the wheel late and nearly miss the turn.

'Are you drunk?'

'Yeah, a bit.'

'There's the house.'

I park the car. The porch light shines down on the wooden steps and the red earth. Ruth walks ahead, opens the door and I carry Jane, asleep.

'Bring her through, up here.'

I walk along the passage and into the bedroom and put her down on a double bed. There is a smell of perfume in the room. Ruth slips the little sandals off Jane, pulls the sheet up over her and comes out into the passage. 'You want a coffee? Come on, I'll make some.'

I stand in the kitchen looking around while she is at the sink filling the jug. A warm breeze blows through the kitchen windows making the faded curtains sway. It is a house built for northern heat and the windows and shutters are open. I see all of it in a kind of swaying haze as if the windows, curtains, lights, floorboards and walls are all moving to settle around the shape and colour of Ruth.

'How do you have it?' She bends down to the cupboard getting cups.

We take the coffee out to the back steps. There is a small wooden landing. Ruth sits down on the boards, rests her back against the wall, stretches her legs out.

'How do you like it?'

'The coffee or the fishing?'

'The fishing. It's rough, isn't it?'

'Not really, it's okay.'

We look down over the lights of the town; they are just a sprinkling of lights really, against the huge darkness between us and the sky. I have no idea of what I can say, just the feeling that she wants it to be rough.

'Well, maybe it is hard. It's different, all the killing. Takes a while to get used to it.'

'Do you like it?'

'Yeah, I like the ocean. I like fishing.'

She's been looking down at the lights and now faces me. 'Do you feel better; do you still feel drunk?'

'Not now. I feel as if I should ask you something.'

She laughs. 'What? What?'

'I don't know. Anything. I think maybe I am still drunk. What about you? Tell me something.'

'About me? There's too much to tell.'

She smiles. I reach out to touch her arm and she takes my hand and holds it firmly. It is a sudden movement that makes her totally in control and as she looks at me her eyes try to explain that she knows how to calm my fears. I touch her hair and she leans towards me. Her neck has a faint smell, a warm smell. My face rests against her neck and hair and I can see the lights below us and far out in the gulf a green light which must be a boat heading south. She draws back for a moment, takes both my hands and looks deep into my eyes. 'It's all right,' she whispers. I don't know; I am not sure what power I can have with her and I don't want her to see that. I feel helpless and weak and wildly excited.

'It's all right,' she says again.

'I know, I know.'

I put my hand at the back of her head, feel the shape of her neck and know, with that simple movement, I have the wheel again and am holding on my chosen course.

We kiss. It is a gentle, tender kiss and over too quickly. I stand, holding Ruth's hand, pulling her up with me. 'I have to go, I have to get the car back.'

'All right,' she says, and we walk into the house again. She carries the cups to the sink and rinses them. The wind blows the curtains at the window. I put my hands on her shoulders, gently, and say, 'I'm sorry.' The tap is running. She stops it and flicks the drops of water from her hands, turns and says, 'It's all right.'

It is after ten o'clock. I'm hungry and walk into the bar to buy something to eat. The place is almost empty now, just a couple of fellows playing darts and another rolling a smoke.

I buy two pies and a beer and go out to the beer garden

and sit down at the same table we'd been at an hour earlier. The beer garden is empty.

There is a faint smell of perfume on my hand and a deep knife cut near my thumb that hasn't healed. The cat that had been around earlier is back, sitting under the table. I touch it with my foot. 'What are you after, kitty?'

Ernie comes out of the door to the main bar where the band is playing. I hear the music for a moment. He sees me and walks over.

'Hey Joe, we're inside. Where's Ruth?'

It's as if he has suddenly realised I'm alone and his face changes as he says, 'You coming?'

'Yeah, let's go.'

Well ... I know where she is. But I wonder why sometimes it seems as if they want you to hurt them to hold them.

The big bar room is smoky and crowded. Over the swaying bodies on the dance floor I can see the lead singer. Ernie pushes ahead, saying something I can't hear. I jostle my way to the bar. The staff are flat out, trying hard to keep up with the pressing, urgent drinkers.

I wait to be served. The dancers on the floor seem to be grasping, holding and thrusting away. The music thumps and soothes. I see the skipper dancing with an older woman. He holds her close and dances slowly at the edge of the crowd. Around him the younger dancers roll and shake as if fighting and loving but he sails quietly, slowly, beside them.

The barmaid brings me a beer and I walk past the edge of the dance floor and see Charlie and Claire dancing right in front of me. 'Hey!'

Charlie sways, smiles, waves and Claire points and I

see Ernie sitting at a table near the wall. I weave my way over to it.

'Where did you get to?' he asks.

Fuckin' hell, good question, Ernie.

'Getting a beer. Where's Martin?'

He nods towards the dance floor. 'Up there somewhere.'

I can't see Martin but Claire is coming, pulling at Charlie's hand. She is flushed and breathless, plucking at her blouse.

'Was Jane okay? Did she stay asleep?' she asks me.

'Sleeping like a lamb.'

Charlie slumps down into a chair. 'Jesus, pass that jug, will you, mate. Bloody dry.'

'And did you stay for a while and she was okay?' Claire is still standing.

I laugh. 'Sit down. Have a drink. Ruth's with her. She's okay.'

She sits down, leans her shoulders right back against the chair, stretches her legs out, arms hanging straight down.

The skipper arrives, guiding the woman he's been dancing with to the table.

Martin walks towards us, smiling, swaying slightly, a beer in his hand.

For two hours we talk, drink, smoke, laugh, get drunker. I have a dance with Claire. It is a song she loves and she jumps up, says to Charlie, 'Oh, come on, come on,' but he is talking to Martin about the fight, so I go with her as she dances towards the dancers, her hand reaching behind for me.

When the band finishes playing the crowd lingers on the floor, calling for another song and the lead singer comes out and they play one more and then it is over, the lights flick on and off and we leave the wreckage on the table and flow out with the crowd into the night.

The skipper has disappeared. There is no sign of Sarge. We stand in a little laughing group near the beer garden. Cars are starting up in the parking area. There are shouts. I hear someone laughing loudly and a girl calls out, 'She's already gone, she's gone with Frank.'

Martin has a carton of beer balanced on his shoulder. 'We going to this party or not?'

'Where is it?'

'Fucked if I know,' he says. 'Charlie knows. Hey, Charlie!'

We cross the carpark. Charlie gets into his car, revs the motor. Claire sits next to him and I slump down alongside her.

'Hang on!' Martin shouts. He climbs in the back with Ernie.

The wheels spin on the gravel, we slide across the car park, come sideways into the cloud of dust, straighten up and fishtail off down the road.

'Charlie!' Claire has fallen against me. She moves her shoulders and shuffles between us.

'Charlie!' she says again.

'Yeeehaaaa,' he shouts. All the car windows are open. The warm night air gushes in around us. I rest my head against the window frame, feeling nothing for the houses and shadows jumping away. I am drunk and gulp the rushing wind and feel Claire press into me when we lean away from the corners; I hear her say again, 'Don't

Charlie … no,' and I can only think how strange it is that she doesn't know that this is her wild rider who can flow through the angles, drop down the swells and rise again, smooth as water over rock … somewhere we leave the road altogether and broadside through gravel and low scrub. Charlie stops singing and I see the wheel spin through his hands; the car grips the road again side on. He slings the wheel to straighten up and yells, 'Hey, Martin, where is this place?'

'Take your next right mate, see the street light? Chuck a right just past it.'

Charlie turns and swings off the road to stop in front of a fence. Set back off the road behind the fence is a house with a bunch of balloons hanging under a dim porch light. A narrow path runs out from the steps under the porch towards us. I see it all quickly and then rest my head and close my eyes. I feel drunk and think I might be sick.

We sit in the car.

'You sure this is the right place?' someone says.

'Dunno, looks like it.'

'Not much action.'

'Give it five minutes, the pub crowd might roll up.'

I am dimly aware of another car pulling up close to my door.

'Hey!' the driver shouts. I look across. It is dark. I can see the outline of his car and a thin gleam of light tracing off the roof, but the voice comes out of darkness. 'Hey, didn't you fuckin' hear me? Is this where the show is?'

I hear him say something else, but I'm not interested. Martin is opening a beer in the back … 'Who else? Joe, you having one? Here, get this into you.'

I don't want another beer but I take the can and say to the voice behind the darkness, 'Is this where the show is, hey? Why don't you go and bloody find out yourself?'

Claire moves away from me. Charlie has put his arm around her and she leans towards him.

'I'm going to sink this can and go in and see what's going on,' Martin says. 'I'm going to go in there and stir the joint up.'

I tilt my can up, take a mouthful and then there is a cracking in my head as if a piece of sharp wood has jammed down behind my eye. I feel only vaguely alive, dimly knowing that someone is wrenching the door open, dragging me out.

I am on the ground, in the dirt, dirt in my mouth, I hear the slam of a car door, the spray of gravel and wheels spinning near me and then Charlie saying, 'Fuck! What the hell! Get him in. Get him in,' leaning over me. 'Joe, Joe. You right, mate?'

Claire puts her arm around me.

'Oh God, God,' she says, and then we are in the car again, moving, her hand gentle and light on the top of my head until we pull up and they lead me towards the house. I want to sit down on the step and I stand not wanting to move, looking down at the solid timbers and blood, two or three drops, like red raindrops on my shoe and on the dark wood.

'We gotta go after him now,' Martin says.

Charlie has his arm around my shoulder. 'We gotta fix Joe up,' he says. 'Come on mate, let's get inside.'

Ruth stands in front of me. She takes my hand and we all go into the house to the bathroom. There is a mirror. I see my eye, dark already, bloody, closing up. I move my jaw, gently. The bone over my eye feels crooked. They are all around me in the little room. The tap is running. There is a pain in my hip. I pull up my bloody shirt.

'Here, let me see,' Claire kneels at my side, looking, saying nothing. My hip is bruised and cut and there are tiny pebbles of gravel stuck in the blood.

'Bastard put the boot in,' Charlie says.

'Jesus!' Martin says.

I see his face in the mirror, saying, 'Come on, let's go and find the mongrel.'

'Here, just face me now,' Ruth says. She has a wet towel and gently dabs it over my eye.

'Just leave him,' I say. 'Don't worry about him.'

'No … we gotta get the bastard,' Martin moves away in the mirror.

I don't want to talk anymore. 'We don't even know who it was.'

Martin says, 'Joe, listen! The bastard's walked over and king hit you through the car window. Christ.'

'But Joe's right, we didn't see him,' Charlie says.

Martin almost laughs. 'Who else would do it? — it's the same big dopey bastard — he thought Joe was me, he was after me, that's what he's done.'

'Look, just leave it,' I say. 'It's finished.'

'Bullshit.' Martin walks out. 'Come on, Charlie.'

I am alone in the bathroom with Ruth and Claire. They are on either side of me with wet towels, Claire kneeling and cleaning my hip and Ruth's face close, wiping gently around my eye. I hear Charlie's car start.

'I'll have to take your shirt off,' Claire says. She eases it off and wipes my chest. There are smears of blood. She rinses the towel and I see a red swirl in the sink.

'That's better.'

I look into the mirror and see my closed eye and feel the strangeness in the bone above it. We all look out at my face. I am framed between the two of them holding me. They are both looking in and looking out, waiting to know how I will see myself. Claire's face and eyes are full of beautiful sadness and Ruth holds the bloody towel; there is blood on the back of her hand.

'It's better now,' she says. 'It will be all right now.'

They hold me and we walk to the kitchen. There is a couch near the wall.

'Here.' Claire sits me down, puts a cushion behind my shoulders.

'Just lie down here.'

Ruth is in the kitchen making coffee. There is the sound of a car like a roar of wind.

'Is that them?' Claire looks over at Ruth.

She pulls a curtain away from the window. 'No, just someone driving past.'

Claire sits alongside me. She strokes my forehead. Ruth brings the coffee and I sit up to drink it. There is a heaviness in my head now. After the coffee I sleep for a little while and then wake and hear the two of them outside on the step, talking quietly. Someone has pulled a rug up over me and my shoes are off.

I sleep again and wake when a car door closes. There are footsteps. Charlie comes in. He turns the light on but I lie still with my eyes closed. He is at the sink getting a glass of water, and then walks down the passage to the bedroom. He is alone.

I lie on the couch on my back with the pale night light

at the windows and gently touch the new, strange shape around my eye.

The house is quiet now. I wonder where Martin is. I think about what the king hit man might look like and whether it was Big Bob and I imagine myself meeting him. There is a sad feeling in me that we don't know each other and I want only to have him look at me and know what is in my eyes and behind them. I want him to see that I am sad because he hadn't wanted to know me and I wonder if he, too, is lying somewhere, broken, thinking.

I think about Ruth and Claire and their hands on me and their gentle eyes and Big Bob and how strange it is that I only want to talk to him, buy him a beer. Come on, come in you crazy bugger! Sit on the end of the couch. Go on! Sit there! Sit there and listen! You hear the silence? Hear them breathing in the other rooms? Yes, they're sleeping now, or maybe Claire's awake, sprawled across the bed, her hand lightly stroking Charlie's hair. And Ruth, across the hallway in the other room. Shall we bring them out? You want them to come so they can show you what they saw in me? You want them to fix you, too? Yes, let's wake all the sleepers! Let's bring them softly from the dark. That's it. Get us all a beer, Bob. Don't look so fuckin' sheepish. Yeah, course I can drink. This is nothing, just a bruise, a crack, blood in my eye. I'll tell you something Bob, you really know how to turn on a good party! Drink up, you bastard. Don't worry about Charlie, he might look as if he wants to thump you, but he'll be all right. Hey, here's my father. Get him a beer. He can tell you a story or two about fighting.

The curtains move lightly at the window and I lay awake

for a long time, feeling warm and cold and with thoughts spinning out at me and then I hear a door open and soft steps in the passage. It is Ruth. There is a cool, pale moonlight she steps through and crosses the room, bends down near me, silently, waiting until she senses that I am awake.

'You all right?' she says. Her hand moves on my hair.

'Yeah, I'm right.'

When she goes I watch the curtains. My mother will want to know. She will be shocked. And Bruno. What will Bruno say? Maybe I can hide it. Yes, I think, perhaps you can bury something of yourself to live well with others, but if you want to be alone ... well, let them see it all.

FIVE

As I write this I can see, out through the window, a misty rain; it is the sort of day for rainbows: big moving lumps of grey-white clouds, patches of blue sky, sunshine, but in the south the sky is blue-black and brooding and I wouldn't be surprised if it moved up over us in an hour or so. Sally has gone to town with Sonny. The house is quiet.

I was about to carry on and describe what happened the following morning — how we went off to unload the boat and the jokes about my black eye, 'Pirate Joe' and all the rest of it — but it doesn't seem important at the moment and I know I'll have no trouble picking it up later on. I've been wondering about secrets and control and the idea of 'burying some part of yourself to live well with others' and I see now that it all started a long time ago and perhaps that is why I was so keen to join Charlie and go back.

Wait! Wait now! The black cockatoos are flying up the hill from the creek. Listen! Hear the screech? See how they swing low over the sloping paddocks? Are they landing? Yes. Behind the trees. In the trees, close. Listen to how their call changes. The harshness has gone. They are feeding now, out of sight, in the trees, like a crowd of children who have run together from their wild play to be handed slices of watermelon. The rain must be closer. (There's an old saying around here that a flock of black cockatoos means rain is on the way.)

What interests me at the moment, more than anything else really, is the idea of the controlled character. Lizzie was controlled, I'm sure of it. Her writing seems honest and steady. I doubt if she even had to work at it.

A few years ago, just before the little bloke arrived, I got involved with theatre. The local group put on a play and with enormous fear I took part.

The rehearsals involved voice control. One night I stood on the stage with the empty hall out in front, it was like being on the boat, behind the wheel, watching the roll of the deck, the navigation lights showing red and green in the spray and the crashing bow sailing on into blackness.

'Project your voice,' I was told. 'Let it reach out through breathing and expression. Let it float to the end of the hall without giving the impression of shouting.'

Clarity of expression. Voice control. Yes, it worked well. We had a full house on the performance night and after the show people looked at me with a shine in their eyes and told me how well I'd done. It made me feel happy, but uneasy: I got the idea into my head that control is all acting ... I'm not sure why this should have bothered me, perhaps it had to do with knowing that my heroes never seemed to be acting at all.

And perhaps I only remember it now because of what happened the other night. Sally came home from work late. She'd been to a meeting and after that to the pub with a friend. She doesn't usually drink a lot but I could tell as soon as she walked in the door that she'd had three, maybe four glasses of wine.

Sonny was asleep. The house had been silent for hours.

She sat down and started to tell me about the meeting and the pub. She was excited, drunk, laughing, breathless. I listened, watching her and then she looked hard at me and said, 'Are you going to tell me what you've been writing about?'

I didn't want to tell her but she wouldn't drop it so I read her a short piece, just half a page. She listened, but I had the feeling she was preoccupied with other thoughts.

When I finished she didn't say anything, just got up, went to the sink, drank a glass of water and walked off to bed.

I thought that would be the end of it, but the next morning she asked me if she could read the whole thing. I felt a thrill of fear and excitement. I told her I didn't think it was a good idea.

She was lying in bed, head propped up on a pillow and I went out to the kitchen to make coffee, took a cup in to her, then gathered up what I'd written and put it on the bed. She propped herself up and started reading and I left her.

A couple of times in the next hour I walked back in as if I was looking for something, but only wanting to see her face. She took no notice of me.

Sonny came out and got a plate for his breakfast. 'Is it Mum's day off?' he asked.

'Sure is, it's the weekend.'

Finally, I went back and Sally was lying on her side;

some pages were on the bed, others on the floor. I thought she was asleep. I waited for her to say something but she didn't.

'Didn't you like it?' I asked.

'I don't want to be involved. It's not me. What's all this living in the past and heavy heart stuff anyway?'

'It's a story.'

She didn't answer so I walked out again but after about a minute I knew what I could say and went back.

'I can make it into our story.'

'Just leave me,' she said.

Her foot was sticking out from under the sheet. I stroked it.

'Don't worry, I'll make you into a superstar, happy endings, the works.'

'You're crazy,' she said. 'But I don't care. Write anything you like, what does it matter?'

'You won't be sorry, I'll paint all your best points in wonderful detail.'

'What best points? You've turned me into a bad girl.'

'Are you serious?'

'Well, you have, I used to go to church; that's all finished now.'

'Did I stop that?'

'Probably.'

Sonny came in. He listens to everything we say.

'Hey, Dad,' he said, 'You know God? Well, before we were born, were we all God and after we die are we all God again?'

'Well, if everyone is a part of God I suppose that could be right.'

Sally gave me a funny look.

'I was thinking about going for a drive,' I said. 'Do you want to come?'

'Not really,' she said, but then looked over at me and asked, 'Where to? The cemetery?'

'No. Why?'

'That's your usual idea of an exciting drive.' And she laughed, in a playful, joking way.

I waited outside at the ute thinking of what she'd said about church. I remembered going myself when I was a boy ... we'd all be outside the house on Sunday mornings with my father, mucking around with the cricket bat, waiting for my mother. She'd be in the house getting ready and then come brightly and quickly out in her best clothes, adjusting her hat and we'd get in the old car and drive past the barking dog and the chooks running, the sunlight and shade across the sandy track to the main road, my father driving us in to the church in our little town and my mother would turn and see one of us on the back seat with a dirty face and lick her fingers and rub our cheeks and then flick her hair and something from his coat as he drove, but he wouldn't notice; he'd be glancing out past the big trees on the edge of the road to the paddocks with the distant look on his face, the same look that was there on Anzac Day mornings at the farmhouse when we'd polish his shoes while my mother searched for a missing war ribbon which, it seemed to me, my father couldn't care less about.

'Don't worry about the ribbons,' he'd say, but she'd always find them and he'd stand stiffly still while she pinned them to his coat and later, in the town, I'd see him march along with the other soldiers and he'd have the same look on his face.

I remember the rain slashing down on the tin roof of the church and the singers battling to rise above the noise. My father did not sing; the look would be on his face, dreamlike, but not detached, as if he were not in the church at all, but somewhere else; a place he'd been, perhaps, or somewhere he wanted to go. And all the kids would kneel during the prayers and muck around and we'd watch our parents walk out to receive the wine. Our eyes were supposed to be closed, praying, but we always watched and wondered about the strange, sacred moment with the bread and wine and the droning tones of the priest: 'This is my body which is given for you. Preserve my body and soul unto everlasting life. This is my blood which is shed for you ...' Hands clasped and lifting. Lips on the silver cup. Drinking the wine, stiff and serious, candles burning, and we'd giggle as old Barnes walked back to his seat, licking his lips, his nose like a tomato and above it all, at the altar, the silence of the priest as we knelt, our heads pressed down on the timber railings. Praying.

The priest would announce the last hymn and we'd all rise to sing, holding our hymn books, all the mothers singing clearly.

I waited and Sonny ran out with Sally behind him. She'd put lipstick on.

It was a crisp morning. Two magpies hopped off the track and flew up onto the low branch of a peppermint tree as we drove out. All the leaves on the trees were clean and shining; when I was a child if someone had told me an elf or fairy had given the leaves a coat of polish during the night with a tiny brush I would have believed it. Maybe someone did tell me.

I could already see how the ocean would look and then we came over the hill and I was right: flat, blue water and the curve of the dark river below us; low tide, brown reefs beyond the beaches like sheets of rust with white strips further out where the waves cracked onto them and then, far away, the sharp line of the horizon.

We dropped down with the road through the hills, steady, solid, but in places near the edge, crumbling to the beaches.

I pulled up at the parking area and there was the river in front of us, trapped now with a sandbar of beach across the bottom of the valley. In the bay the waves broke and washed up the shore and spray flew when they hit the black rocks.

'That's Old Man Rock,' I said.

'Where?'

'Down this end, in the corner. See the swell coming now, just about to break over it? There! That rock.'

'What's Old Man Rock, Dad?'

'There's an Aboriginal story about it.'

'How come we've never heard it before?' Sally asked.

'Don't know,' I said.

We sat in the ute and watched the ocean and the beach and the hills.

'Well, what's the story?' Sally asked.

'There was an Aboriginal leader. He made the river. He had a daughter who wanted to run away with the man she loved so she stole her dad's magic stick and ran away. But he chased her all along the river and when they reached the ocean she hit him with the magic stick and he fell into the sea and turned into that rock. Old

Man Rock. Come on … let's go for a walk.'

We walked on the beach and the rocks and Sonny saw some crabs in a crack and a few small fish in a pool.

When we got back to the ute Sally said, 'Look at that.'

A few hundred metres out past the rocks where the water changed to a deep blue I saw the spray of a whale.

'It's a whale.'

'Where?'

I lifted Sonny up and sat him on the bonnet. 'Wait a minute. There! See the spray?'

We watched for ten minutes and I looked down at the river and the beach and remembered a short entry in Lizzie's diary about a whale washed up at the mouth of the river and how she'd come here on her horse with a few others to boil the whale flesh and make oil for the lamps.

I pictured the scene as I stood looking down: horses waiting, tied to scrubby bushes at the edge of the beach; Lizzie working with a group of men, stoking the fires, hacking out lumps of whale flesh, prodding the drums; her long dress tucked up, arms smeared with whale fat, the sun going down, darkness, white water breaking on Old Man Rock; Lizzie wiping a strand of hair from her forehead, carrying a slab of blubber to the fires, a spray of sparks, the dark shape of the whale near the water; walking to her horse, riding home in the night through the coast hills and into the heavier bush until she reached the hut, sitting down tired in her room, the quietness of the night outside settling, gently stroking her hair and then dipping the nib in the ink to begin.

It was all spread out in front of me: the beach, the waves, Old Man Rock, the river …

'Shall we go?' Sally asked.

'Has the whale gone away now?' Sonny asked.

'Can't see him,' I said.

'Or her,' Sally said.

I started the old ute and on the drive back thought about work and silence and Lizzie and the whale … the silence after long hard work; Lizzie smeared with whale oil, tired, alone, the lamp flickering into her still world and because I was so close to it again, I felt the silence after killing turtles: sitting on the gunwale, smoking, blood dried on our arms and no one speaking until someone would say, 'Bit fuckin' rough out there today,' and I thought about the whale on the beach becoming part of Lizzie's silence; the hacked carcass alone on the night's pale shore had come to her world of quiet and tired bones just as it did after we unloaded the boat and saw the sick whale again as we headed north for the islands with the skipper at the wheel and the blokes happy after our break in the town, all joking and excited out on the deck, teasing me about my black eye until the skipper shouted, 'There's that sick whale,' and we saw, a hundred metres away, the oily water and the smooth dark shape rolling. When he angled the boat over we saw the sharks, their fins breaking the surface and going under the heavy smoothness of the whale.

'What's wrong?' Sally asked, as we came in under the trees hanging over the track and I stopped the ute near the house.

'What do you mean?'

'Are you in a funny mood?'

'No, just thinking about the whale.'

'Look,' she said, 'don't get the wrong idea from what I said about the story, it's just that I don't know if anyone can tell the real story and even if you could I can't think why you'd want to.'

'It's only a story.'

'No it's not, it's about us.' She was silent and then looked at me. 'What's all this heavy heart business anyway?'

Well, she would wonder, I suppose. And why shouldn't she? It's not as if I'd sat down and explained the thing to her. I couldn't explain it to myself, really. I suppose I didn't want to. Didn't really want to track it down. Who wants to go after a slow, creeping, bastard of a feeling that they've lost their passion? I couldn't give her an honest answer; I wasn't ready, didn't know how to. And, most of all, I didn't want to reach out and drag her towards whatever it was I'd become.

'I don't know,' I said. 'It's not the end of the world. I'm going to town to buy some smokes. Is there any money?'

She didn't answer so I got out of the car and walked into the house and started to look around for loose change in all the usual places. Sonny had followed me in and I saw his face crumple as I walked out to the car again. Sally was still sitting in there and I reached over her to get into the glovebox.

When the ute started Sally got out and I drove towards town thinking about the sick whale again and the grey shapes and dark shadows of the sharks and the thrashing and blood in the water and how Charlie and I had watched as we cruised slowly past and how he'd said, 'Wonder why they took so fuckin' long to hit him?'

I bought the smokes, drove home again, went in and

sat on the verandah. The house was quiet; I didn't know where she was, maybe in the bedroom with Sonny; I felt as if I couldn't move my head, just locked in, staring straight ahead at an empty beer bottle on the table in front of me, flicking my ash into it and then I heard the door open and she came out and said, 'What's wrong, Joe?' and everything in her voice spread into me like water over parched earth and I started to cry without any cares about crying, not like those times when you can force a moment of sadness because you want them to see it — no, I couldn't hide; it was simply there, breaking and loose and couldn't be covered any more and there weren't even any thoughts of how dangerous it might be or how it would shake her and I dumbly scratched at the label on the beer bottle as if something else was in control of my fingers. After a while I ran my hands over my face and hair as if I'd just come up from a dive and I stood up and saw what was in her eyes and went over, put my hand on her shoulder and said, 'It's all right, it's all right.'

Later in the night the rain came. I wasn't surprised. Two days earlier the flying ants had come into the house at night and floated around the light and I'd seen them land on the table, shed their wings and walk away. There were tiny silky wings all over the place.

I woke after the rain stopped. It was dripping from the gutters and I lay in bed looking out through the window at the dark until a tiny smear of pale light came into the east as if someone had walked out draped in a sheet and dropped it where the earth meets the sky and walked on into the darkness.

I slipped my leg over so it touched Sally's. She was

warm and smooth and there was a flashpoint of warmth, so close and fragile that the only movement I could make would break it; I knew that the breaking would be like a fire going out in dark rain, so I stayed close for a long time and then pulled away and sat up in bed, shaking. The white sheet was gone; it had spread into cold dawn light.

In the morning she asked, 'What time are you leaving?'

We were in the kitchen. I waited for the toast as she poured the coffee. She was dressed, ready for work, make-up on, little silver droplet earrings, shiny black shoes, a deep red-coloured skirt and a neat black jacket.

'About ten o'clock.'

Sonny came out; he'd just woken and walked straight past both of us without speaking and through the door onto the verandah. He was after something.

I followed him. The car was parked in the driveway under the spreading branches of the peppermint tree and he walked to it, barefoot, and opened the door.

I waited near the house, watching. He came back towards me, holding something.

'What is it?'

He looked up, held his hand out to show me. It was a little toy animal, some sort of plastic kangaroo.

Sally came out carrying her briefcase. 'I'm off to work. I'm late. Drop Sonny on your way through town.' She bent down and kissed him, then leaned towards me and we kissed quickly.

'Better come in and have some breakfast,' I said to Sonny. He was squatting on the path playing with his toy.

We went into the house and I started throwing a few

clothes into a bag and Sonny looked up from the table, holding his spoon and said, 'Where are you going?'

'I'm going to Perth, be back tomorrow. I'll drop you off at Mum's work and she'll take you to child care and pick you up later.'

'Why are you going to Perth? Can I come?'

'No, not this time. I just have to do some things.'

There was no solid reason for the trip. I'd told Sally I just wanted to wander around, see a movie, buy a couple of books; I hadn't been to the city for a while and it was over a year since I'd gone alone. Sally goes a lot. She has meetings and work commitments.

I got my gear together and a few things for Sonny and just before ten o'clock drove to town, dropped him off with Sally, waved goodbye, tooted the horn and swung out onto the main road, down past the karri trees, over the bridge, across the river and up the hill on the way north, out of town.

As I drove I kept thinking about Sonny. For the first forty kilometres, driving on the black road past the farms behind the fences, with cows grazing in the paddocks, I thought about how he'd walked towards the car to get his toy and how he'd looked, walking slowly, deliberately, almost blindly; seeing nothing except what he was hoping to find and what he could do with it.

I was going over all of the old country now and came into the flatlands and farms on the outskirts of Busselton, driving north in the morning to the city, the windows open, the late spring paddocks with a new green after the hay cutting, the big yellow rolls of hay and, coming up now on my left, a driveway with a farmhouse and sheds at the end, that I looked closely at, remembering, because a few years earlier I'd driven past this place in winter rain and seen a young farm girl walking the cattle along the track for the afternoon milking; her hair was straggly and wet as she followed the cows; her gumboots looked too big; she was a child walking without a dream, lonely, sad and lovely in the rain.

I drove through Busselton with the old train in the park and then out along the straight road, flanked on each side with the neat lines of poplar trees and north again through the tuart forest. (I love the way the big trees tower up over the road and their shadows are dappled across it.) Lizzie probably rode her horse under these trees; it's only twenty miles from the place she grew up, the first old homestead, and she covered a lot of country on horseback when she was a girl. On past the pine plantation and then back to the main road again with the smoke stacks, piles of dirt, conveyor belts and machinery of the sand mine outside Capel and the ripped earth and dams alongside the highway, the pumps and pipes and dirty water.

After the Bunbury roundabout the new double lane highway swept north and I turned the radio on. Talkback radio. People ringing in and discussing issues: crime in the city, law and order, the drug problem; occasionally someone rang with a humorous solution to a serious problem.

It felt good to be out on the road with the sun and wind and trees. Surely the waves are clean, I thought, breaking crisp over the reefs today. Clean and blue lifting swells, smoking along the tops with the breeze. I felt excited thinking about the drive to the city and about Sally and me. It was a moment of coming out of uncertainty so sharply that I was reminded of the grace and swiftness of a dropping eagle: what was ahead was clear and coming up fast and everything behind was where I had come from and belonged and where I could return to with a soaring swoop.

Not long after the whale and the sharks, Charlie and I are alone together in the fo'c'sle; he is polishing his gun with a rag and oil and his brown legs hang loosely over the bunk; the gun is cradled in his lap. He likes to look after his gear well; knives, guns, cars. I watch him with his little oil tin, carefully pouring a lidful onto the rag to rub lovingly into the rich coloured timber of the stock. The gun is a 30.30 Winchester. He wraps the oily rag around the barrel and slowly pulls it through; the dull blue metal gleams. He lifts the rifle, nestles it into his shoulder, closes an eye and sights along the barrel towards the fo'c'sle hatch.

The boat gently rises and falls; the rest of the crew are down on the aft deck and it is unusual for the two of us to be alone together.

'Here, give us a look.'

He passes the rifle over and I rock the weight of it in my hands and open and close the bolt a couple of times.

'It's a bloody nice rifle.'

He doesn't say anything. I'd used the gun before a couple of times; once when we'd taken the dinghy and left it on the beach and walked up into the foothills of the ranges and shot a goat. We'd carried it back to the dinghy, pushed off at the shore, started the outboard motor and punched out through the chop to the main boat. Charlie had said, 'Make a nice change from fuckin' turtle meat,' as his foot rested on the white goat, red near the neck where the bullet had come out.

I pass the rifle back and he wraps it into a long grey bag and slips the whole package down at the side of his bunk.

'My old man had a .303.'

'Yeah, I know,' he says. 'You told me.'

Charlie tugs and fiddles with his hair. Talking about my father always makes him uneasy.

He pushes a pillow under his head and stretches out on his bunk, staring up at the poster of a naked girl he has stuck to the ceiling of the deck above his head; he could have reached up and touched her.

I can see why he might have been wary about my father: I remember the two of us riding our horses and I'd say, 'Let's call around to my place for a while and give the horses a drink before we head to the pub,' and we'd tie our horses to a small tree outside the house and I'd go in and my dad would come back out with me to watch the horses drinking and he'd say hello to Charlie; we'd toss the reins over and swing up into the saddle and my father would have the look on his face which Charlie saw, but did not understand, because it was full of longing and love and sad wonder about our reckless ways.

I look over and say, 'How long do you reckon it'd take those sharks to finish off the whale?'

'Stuffed if I know,' he says. 'Every shark in the gulf will be headed flat out over there; big highway straight to the feast.'

'Yeah.'

'That's their favourite pastime.'

'Remember that shark with the babies? The one we cut open?'

He rolls onto his side.'Yeah. Tough little fellers.'

A couple of years earlier we'd strung a wing of net out from the beach at night. In the morning a shark was rolled and tangled close to shore. We'd dragged it into the shallow water. It was a dead female with a heavy sagging belly. 'Full of little ones,' Charlie had said and I watched as he pushed the knife in, made a long slit and out rolled the baby sharks in their clear, slimy sacs. He'd nicked the filmy skin and slid them out; perfectly formed baby sharks about a foot long. We'd held them in the clear water until they shivered alive and their tails swung gently as they swam away.

'Probably a couple of those little fellers feeding on that whale right now,' Charlie says.

'You reckon?'

'Could be.'

It was nice driving, remembering. I came down a hill and glimpsed the south end of the Peel Inlet away on my right; a shine of silver water through the trees. I switched the radio off; I hadn't really been listening.

I drove onto the long rising approach to the Dawesville Cut and the new bridge where the channel went through from the inlet to the ocean, and I could see the blue water away to my left and in the eastern distance the soft purple of the Darling Ranges and it was all so easy now to slip back into.

Charlie rolls on his bunk, faces me and says, 'What do you think of Ruth?'

'She's all right.'

He smiles. 'You're a dark horse, you bastard.'

'Bullshit.'

'Well, you like her, don't you?'

'Yeah, she's nice.'

'She reckons you're all right.'

'How do you know?'

'Word gets out.'

'Is that what Claire said?'

He smiles, turns his head, looks up at the poster again.

We are both quiet for a while and then he says, 'I met a feller in town we used to work with; Morgan.'

'I remember him.'

'Reckons there's a big job starting down south soon. Told him I might have a look after the season's over.'

'Plenty of driving work?'

'Yeah, heaps.'

I remember our first job together and going early each morning from the camp with the rest of the team on the back of a ute out to where we were working. We would jolt to the top of a red pindan hill and below us was the flat stretch of spinifex plain with the line of another red hill running across it in the distance and more hills further out, dark parallel shadows across the land. On the first flat stood the yellow machines silent and waiting and the red scars over the earth where we'd been ripping dirt to build the road.

We'd jump from the ute and walk over to the machines, the scrapers, dozers, graders and water tanks with their shadows long across the spinifex in the early morning silence. All day Charlie and I would wheel our scrapers into the pit, drop the belly plate down into the red dirt and kick the throttle hard, fill the bowl with spilling earth, snap the apron shut and roar out again, gaining speed until we galloped like crazed beasts to spill and spread our loads along the new road.

We'd drive barefoot, passing close in clouds of dust and I'd see his face caked with red and his white teeth and at night we'd go to our tent and sit on the dirt drinking a beer, talking with the older men and feeling good. We were seventeen, the youngest in the camp, and we were building a part of the new road north with some of the old 'guns', the legends; one night as we sat outside the tent, Morgan said to us, 'You young blokes want to take it easy on those fuckin' scrapers. You know what they call 'em, don't you?'

'What?'

'Widowmakers.'

Charlie is lying with his eyes closed. He seems asleep.

'So what about Claire and Jane, if you go back on the machines?' I ask.

'Yeah. Don't know. Haven't worked it out yet, could always get a caravan. Maybe they'll stay in Perth. Just wait and see what happens.'

He jumps off the bunk, climbs the fo'c'sle ladder and puts his head out through the hatch.

'Can you see the islands?'

'Yeah, we're about an hour away.'

I am back there again, seeing the clean beaches and the afternoon sun lighting the scrub on the low hills of the island as we watch from the deck, slicing through the blue water with the creamy bow wave spreading away, but I am coming into Mandurah, too, and feel hungry so I turn off at the lights and drive to the nearest takeaway chicken place, buy some chicken and chips and stand outside, leaning against the car, eating.

An hour to the city. An hour to the islands. I chuck my scraps in a plastic bin and drive out to join the traffic.

There are two islands. A narrow channel of water separates them. We come into it and drop the anchor where the top end of the south island scoops out into a little bay. We are only a hundred yards from the shore with five fathoms of blue water under us.

An hour later the two dinghies are tied to a clump of oyster rock halfway along the south island. Martin and Charlie are perched on the rock opening oysters with their knives. Ernie and I are sitting in the dinghies. 'What are we going to do?' he asks me.

Charlie looks over, spits out a bit of oyster shell and says, 'Nothing we can do. There's stuff all turtles here. You come out to these islands, they're either here or they're not. How long we been fishing? Three hours? For one turtle.' He bends over to prise open another oyster with his knife. 'You cover that much ground out here and only see one turtle, must be nothing here. Just have to go back and tell him to move on.'

The skipper stands on the deck looking out at the island and the ocean. 'You went right to the south end?'

'The whole way.'

'And nothing at all?'

'No. No tracks on the beaches. Nothing in the water.'

'What about the weed country?'

'Covered all of it. Bugger all there.'

He is silent. The sun has gone down and the pink light of dusk has spread into the sky.

'We'll head back to the west coast first thing in the morning,' he says. 'Might be able to get a few snapper off the deck tonight.'

Sarge takes the freezer hatch off and climbs down and then up again with frozen vegies and bread. 'You fellers get a couple of quick ones and I'll cook 'em up with this,' he says.

Ernie gets a line over the side first and catches a good sized snapper before the rest of us have started. There is a lump of red turtle meat thawing out on the deck. I thread a piece onto the hook so the barb is clear and toss it out. The line is old, well used and the slack lies flat on the deck. The tide is not strong and I can feel the weight of the bait slowly sinking.

After a minute the weight of the line begins to slowly drag across my fingers. 'Bit touchy,' Ernie says to me. The movement stops, just for a moment and then it is back again, a smooth, sucking weight and the line draws out steadily faster and now I can feel a strength behind it and I pull back and all of the weight is there and for a second no line is lost or gained, it is a moment for both the fish and me of finding out who has the advantage and what to do with it. The line goes out fast, almost burning my hand but I stop the run, holding, and I feel the fish doing the same; holding hard, and I can picture the curve of blue and silver, fighting, locked into position.

I gain some line and bring it steadily in using only my fingers and thumbs, gently, not letting it slip into any cracks. The fish pulls away again with a short, hard run but I turn it, close to the boat, almost to the surface and then it swims for the bottom, straight down, but it comes up again and splashes on the top and I swing it up over the gunwale and down onto the deck. It is a big snapper, maybe ten pounds. I slide my hand in behind the gills and twist the hook out.

'He's a fuckin' beauty mate,' Charlie says, holding his line, waiting, and then he leans forward, tense, arm stretched out and almost whispers, 'Hold it boys, hang on me old shipmates, I do believe he's having a sniff. That's it, sniff around old feller, have a decent bite, bloody good tucker, slip right into it. Go on.' And he strikes hard, pulling in wildly, elbows up and swinging, teeth biting his bottom lip.

'Don't pull his head off, mate,' Ernie says. But Charlie is not listening. He holds the line with both hands, not gaining or losing.

'Fiery little colt,' he says. 'Come on old feller, come on me little mate.'

He leans over the gunwale and swings the snapper up onto the deck.

'Hungry old timer,' he mutters. 'Swallowed the bloody hook.'

We fish for an hour, lined up along the gunwale, and there are over twenty snapper in the red baskets and then, suddenly, they are not biting any more and we begin the filleting.

'That was better than a kick in the arse,' Ernie says.

The skipper wipes his knife. 'That's the way to catch them. No mucking around. Straight on the hook.'

'Good size too.'

'Yeah. Good fillets. Nice bit of booze money.'

Later at night, sitting on my bunk, I think about writing a letter to Ruth, but I can't, of course, unless I throw it over in a bottle. What could I say to her, anyway?

I make a few notes in my little book and after a while it turns into a poem.

'Who you writing to?' Charlie asks.

I close the book. 'Just getting down a few notes.'

'See you in the morning,' he says, 'I'm going to sleep.'

I look at his back and shoulders. He is dark brown from the sun and his matted hair is golden at the back of his neck. He is upset. There are times he can't get any closer to me and this is one of them. It isn't anger. That's different. This is how he is with my books, too: I have a couple of poetry books on the shelf and sometimes at night when I get them down to read, Charlie will become quiet and wary. It is as if he doesn't want to get too close to some secret in himself. It is strange, because there are other times, when he is drunk and his head tilts over so the ash from his smoke falls into his lap and his ropey hair flops down, that he'll jolt back to life, look at me with the most gentle eyes in the world and say, 'How you going there Joey, you fuckin' old bastard.'

I was driving past the Kwinana refinery now where the tall stacks blow ragged white smoke. The freeway to the city was coming up on my right but I made a snap decision not to take it and waited for the coast road to Fremantle. I turned off and had the ocean on my left. There was a little holiday camping place up ahead with a ramshackle roadside building and a couple of old signs: Eats, Coke, that sort of thing; I'd seen it before but never stopped.

I pulled over, got out, bought a pie and a can of drink and drove down the little track between the holiday huts and parked at the end. The flat ocean was calm as a lake. There was an old ship not far away, near the shore; it looked grounded and rusted. Between me and the water was a narrow strip of sand. The factory stacks with the blowing smoke were further south.

There was no sign of life around the little huts, but I knew it would be a special place for people at holiday time; there would be families, I thought, who've come here for years; the kids would tumble out of the car, Dad would unload the boot while Mum carried camping gear into the hut: fishing rods, chairs, buckets, balls, games, clothing, food.

It was good not to have to hurry, to sit there thinking about how strange it was to come to a new place for the first time, a place that was like a special home.

The whole settlement was as peaceful as the flat, quiet ocean. Everything seemed to have stopped. A piece of loose corrugated iron flapped lazily on one of the huts.

I watched the sun getting lower. It would set in about an hour. I wondered what Sally and Sonny were doing. She would have picked him up from child care now, they'd be back at the house. Sally was probably sitting down with a glass of wine listening to his tales of the day's events. I'll ring her when I get to Fremantle, I thought.

I started the car and drove out, the sun coming through on patches of ocean as I passed the old tanning factories with the smell of hides reminding me of cows after rain, steamy and rich in the dairy when I was about Sonny's age, my father putting a bucket of water down, splashing the cow's udder, milking quietly while the rain poured down like a constant shower of gravel on the corrugated iron roof of the shed so we could barely hear and coming down through the peppermint trees; heavy grey rain marching steadily through the trees making them dark and the bush beyond blurred, driving me down into cold loneliness. Once, I remember, he came to me, took my hand, spread an old hessian bag out in front of the fire under the copper and I sat on it while he milked, watching the red coals and feeling the heat on my legs and hands.

There were boat-building yards on my left now and ramps with boats out of the water, some anchored offshore. I saw a big, new-looking twin-hulled vessel floating quietly.

I followed the coast along, past the pens with hundreds of yachts, their masts bristling across the low sun.

'We have an upstairs room, a single,' the barman said.

'That sounds good.'

He smiled and went into a little side office and came back with the key.

'Fix it up now?' I asked.

'Later is fine,' he said.

'Thanks.'

I ordered a beer and sat looking around and quietly drinking. There were two men at the end of the bar; they looked like truckies and seemed out of place. The pub was very old but had been done up. The polished wood of the bar curved around past me to finish near an open door and I could see two pool tables in another room with a chalk board. There was a counter meal menu up behind the bar.

Another man came in, sat on a stool near me, ordered a beer and started to roll a smoke. He was about fifty and had an interesting face and long, grey, straggly hair.

The barman walked back past me, saw my empty glass and nodded at it, lifting his eyebrows.

'Yeah, righto, thanks.'

He brought me another beer.

'On holidays?' he asked.

'Just up for the night; from down south.'

'Whereabouts?'

I told him and he said, 'Lovely country down that way.' He seemed very relaxed, experienced. Either he's the boss or he's really good at his job, I thought. As he passed again he said to the straggly-haired fellow, 'You check room twenty-three, Col?' The fellow nodded.

I finished my beer and walked out through the big door and onto the street. It was dusk and the old buildings, some of them limestone, looked pale in the soft light. Cars were passing along the street almost within spitting distance of the pub's front door. There was a breeze and I could smell the sea. I stood there, watching the traffic and people walking on the far side of the street. There was a mood of hurrying people; workers heading home, I supposed. The soft sky, high and deep and gentle, slowly gathered back its light.

I walked over to where I'd parked, got in the car and drove around to the back of the pub. The alleyway was narrow with potholes, and dark, down between two high walls. I pulled up, grabbed my bag and found a side door to the hotel and went in. There was a carpeted lounge area and I saw the pool tables from a new angle and beyond them glimpsed the barman and Col; if you'd put a frame around Col you could have called it 'Thinking man with cigarette'.

A wide, carpeted staircase with a richly polished wooden rail rose in absolute silence ahead of me. I walked up, floating my hand along the smooth timber. My room had a little balcony and I leaned on the rail and looked across the street at the old building on the other side. The last of the sky's light was fading to darkness and the streetlights were on.

I watched a woman with two young children waiting to cross. There were a few cars passing. She held one child's arm, holding him back. And then they both moved with her as she hurried them across.

I went into the bedroom and lay on my back on the bed. The walls of the room were bare; it was simply furnished, clean and quiet. I could hear the cars outside but they weren't distracting; they were only small rushes of sound coming into the silence.

After a while I got up and went down the stairs and out to the street. I found a little cafe and sat down and had something to eat and then walked along the street looking in the shop windows. Most of the shops were closed but I came to a bookstore with display stands on the pavement, the door wide open and soft music playing. There were no other customers. The girl running the place sat at the far end, partly hidden behind book stands. She looked at me and smiled.

I browsed around. There were a lot of interesting books and I found a stack of new edition classics for two dollars each and bought a couple. The girl put them in a paper bag.

'When do you close?' I asked.

'About nine,' she said, 'or when people stop coming in.'

The street seemed to be getting busier; a few family groups strolled around, probably out for a meal.

I thought of going down to the small boat harbour, but knew I'd get there later on.

A family crossed the street and went into a restaurant in front of me. The kids were excited. It must have been a special night out for them. I looked quickly up and down the street for a phone box but couldn't see one, otherwise I'd have rung Sally right then. Instead, I took the books back to my room and then went downstairs.

Col, the straggly-haired fellow glanced over at me as I sat down.

I ordered a beer. I wanted to say something to him. It seemed silly, sitting in silence, but he was so settled, so much a part of the place, that for me to speak would have been like stepping in and adjusting the picture of the yachts on the wall behind the bar.

After my second beer I said, 'You live around here?'

He turned his face towards me but his hand, holding his cigarette up as if he were about to throw a dart, remained perfectly still.

'In the pub.'

'This pub?'

He nodded. 'Live and work here.'

There was something slightly off balance about him: perhaps it was the hair; his face was so strong and square that you expected thick, short hair.

I was going to ask if I could buy him a beer but he was drinking very slowly. At times he rolled his lips together and it took something away from his steadiness; it was a quick furtive moment and I noticed too, that the lip rolling was accompanied by a glance around the bar as if he'd just heard a sound that reminded him of something. But, just as quickly, it would pass and he'd be back to his steadiness, making it hard to really accept that his mood had been ruffled.

The beer was making me feel excited and happy. I tried to think of something to say to Col. He seemed a long way away with his thoughts, but he'd smiled at me earlier. He had a nice smile.

'You ever been on them?' I asked.

He was looking up at the picture of the yachts.

'What? Those? No.'

In the picture, two sleek white yachts were tacking, their bows half-buried in blue breaking swell. He kept looking at them, silently, and I thought he'd slipped back to whatever place he'd been in. I expected him to stay quiet, but then he said, 'You see a lot of yacht fellers come in here. Always after something.'

I didn't know what to say. He put his beer down and went on, 'Well, we all chase, don't we? What about you?'

'Yeah ... not sure.'

'You know,' he said, 'I'll tell you something. A friend of mine said to me once, "Col, I'll tell you what you're good at. You're good at taking hold of those moments when a smile is just beginning to replace a grimace and helping them to be born".'

It seemed like a funny thing for an Australian with long straggly hair to be telling me. I'd thought of him as one of those fellows who's had a rough life and now spends his twilight years as a general hand around the pub: permanent room upstairs, bit of bar and cleaning work, that sort of thing. And I wasn't sure if what he'd said was really meant for me but when I saw his eyes full of kind, steady friendliness, I realised it was.

'Well,' I said, lifting my beer, 'cheers anyway.'

He nodded.

A Salvation Army man, in uniform and holding a collection tin, walked up to us. He must have known Col, and with a quiet word he smiled, leaned down and took a coin from the little pile on the bar. He turned to me and I handed him a dollar and he slipped it into the tin and moved on.

'Seems like you're a good customer,' I said.

Col nodded, 'Standard arrangement. He's not selling me anything. I give him a couple of bob, he takes it.'

'What do you think about it?' I asked.

'The Salvos?'

'Yeah.'

I wanted to know a bit more. Maybe he might take it further. His comment about grimaces and smiles had really opened the door, but I still wasn't game to just barge right in.

'They do their job,' he said. 'They represent a truth they believe in.' He looked at me. 'You're not against this imaginary stuff anyway, are you?'

When he said that, I wasn't expecting what happened. I felt as if he'd torn a curtain away from a window and distant blurs were beginning to take shape.

'No, I'm not,' I said.

I saw the Salvo man on the other side of the room. Jesus Christ. I didn't know what else to say to Col. I wanted to say something big.

'It's not something that troubles me,' he was saying now. 'God as an imaginative condition, I mean.'

I was getting drunk and ordered another beer. Col was speeding it up for me, or his words were. But I wasn't really ready for all of the God stuff. I knew there was some sort of link … something to do with the imagination and the thing I'd thought about with Lizzie's simple words, but more than anything I just wanted him to believe he'd made me happy. That was his mission, but Christ, what was he saying? That he was happy with the idea of God as an imaginative truth? I think so. He suddenly stood up.

'Well, that's all for me young man,' he said, looking into his glass, before drinking what was left. He took his tobacco and loose change from the bar, stood up, faced me deliberately and squarely and put out his hand. We shook hands. He didn't smile. I did.

'See ya,' I said and he walked through the bar, going out past the pool tables towards the stairs.

I sat there for a while longer, finishing my beer and feeling warm and light and thinking about him and then I got up and went outside. I was quite drunk.

Lots of people, mainly young people, were on the street now, walking quickly, excited; girls in fashionable clothes chatted and tossed their hair, heading for pubs, I suppose, where the bands were playing, or maybe nightclubs. What time do nightclubs open? Bit early yet, maybe.

There were couples holding hands, swinging along, and others moving more slowly looking into shop windows and young men in twos and threes; all moving through the lights on the gleaming street, moving somewhere in the dark and I moved with them, happy to have fallen into the flow of the night river — it would take me to the sea — others might jump up on the banks earlier, getting off at different stops, opening the doors to old and new places.

I came to a window with a display of boots and saddles, bridles and hats. I stopped and looked for a while and when I went on there were two girls walking past and I fell into step with them. They were about nineteen, bouncing along, laughing, talking. I was caught in the shining bubble of a mood they floated in; I felt part of them and I said, 'You two look happy!'

'We are!' they said in a burst of bright laughter.

'You look as if you're about to light up the whole night.'

For a moment they had seen that I was with them but then I saw a sudden, hard change in their eyes: it was a startled, fearful look. They pressed closer to each other and with quick steps, almost stumbling into a run, moved away from me, looked back once, but I had stopped; I felt sick and breathed hard to stop it coming too quickly because it came like death; a smack at the heart and then the fact behind the shock moving in me.

I sat down on a little street bench and saw them far ahead now, still walking quickly. In that time on the seat I might have been in a dark sea, drifting.

My thoughts sank and rose and swirled me on my little bench until I began to settle and see again. Fifty metres away, on the pavement, a cluster of young people waited outside a building. A man stood near the door, taking money, checking ID.

I sat there trying to make it all right but a cold idea about the hearts of the young slid into me. Something had clouded their view, surely; a shadow had passed across their eyes so that they saw only the grey, the dark.

I got up and walked slowly on and turned down a street past old buildings. I was away from the action of the main strip now; it was quiet and dark as I came to that part of the city that I'd known well years earlier; I was close to the fishermen's harbour and it was all familiar: the street, the park in front of me, the cry of the seagulls.

There was a cool wind off the ocean as I crossed the street and stepped onto the grassy park. I hunched my jacket hard around me and pushed my hands deep in the pockets, walking under the pine trees.

I walked back now to the place we'd first sailed from; I came again to the real places: the old railway tracks I'd crossed with Charlie going from the boat to the pub, the timbers of the wharf, the big rocks on the lee side of the groyne, the water murky and still around the pylons, the fish and chip shop, the birds, and right now I was nearly at the place the boat had been tied when we'd slipped the ropes before dawn on that first morning, stood together on the deck and smoothly moved away from the sheltered water and out into the open ocean.

I was going back to something old and new; already I'd come a long way but now these places warmed me in the cool night.

Charlie had led me back to this place, I suppose. Well, I'd come alone, but he was waiting and now, as I walked, he came to me again from death and I remembered. It was years ago, but he came clearly as I passed the old shop on the waterfront and saw the dark water. It was as if we'd come brown and dusty from the red plains, ready to plunge together into water; as if we'd left the noise of machines far away and wanted to hear only the quiet swish of water passing. His death made me remember the red hills. I could see him, foot to the floor, ride the wild machine into the pit, drop the belly plate, surge down through the gears and come away, earth spilling out, spread the load, gather speed, turn back towards the hills. I could see him riding as it began to buck and twist and roll until out flying he went, down into the dirt with a shadow over him and then the machine falling like a horse that has been shot … down, down on his golden hair … but that is only guessing. I didn't see him die. It was in the hills. He was on a scraper. I got the message one hot afternoon. 'Charlie's been killed on a scraper.'

At the funeral one of his workmates told me it happened just after smoko. Maybe he started to slide. Perhaps he skimmed the bowl too deep trying to stop her. They're bastards once they start bucking. I doubt if he would have chucked it into 'angel gear'. I saw that happen once; a bloke 'let her go' on a big hill, got up too much speed, dropped the bowl and it bucked and jack-knifed and then went end over end.

The workers 'passed the hat around' for Charlie, or for Claire and Jane, I suppose. The last time I saw her was at the funeral. She was rocking gently: her anchor to everything had been jarred and loosened and she rocked quietly, holding on. It was a new rhythm for her, all that she had was still there, but it moved differently in her. She was like a tree in a storm, bent over, but hanging on, graceful and strong in the terrific winds.

There were dull lights in some of the boats across the water as I walked closer. Alongside me was the pale rocky wall, humped up at the dark sky. I could see the shape of boats sitting still on the calm water and the silhouette of others across the harbour and then I came to the place and I sat down with my back against one of the sturdy timber bollards, hung my legs over the edge and looked down at the water. I could make out the opening not far away where the rock wall ended and the sheltered water curved away into the open ocean.

A light, cool breeze blew from the south-east. I remembered how the boat had moved slowly, gliding, and how I'd seen Charlie watching Claire as she began to walk away.

I sat on the dark wharf with the traffic sound and lights of the streets across the water and, for the first time, wondered if he'd had time to know. But even if he had, what would he have known anyway? What may have moved in his heart in the brief, blinding time before it stopped?

Someone stepped from a boat and onto the wharf about fifty metres away and walked into the shadows. A skipper doing some final preparations I suppose. He'd be back in the morning, early. What time would it be, I wondered. Probably close to midnight. The Southern Cross had reached a peak and was beginning its arc back down.

We'd sailed from here, knowing only that somewhere, coming with the sunlight, there would be colours and new country. And the shadow swept away now and the colours sprang again.

Would he have had time to be afraid, I wondered. Was he ever afraid? Yes. But not afraid to show it; and I remembered the dinghy sinking.

'They might be coming tonight,' Charlie says.

  'The girls?'

157

'Yeah.' He's smiling.

'Jesus. You sure? What about the dinghy?'

'We can get it. I asked the skipper. He's okay about it.'

It is sunset. There are thin red streaks high in the west as if someone with bleeding fingers has raked a hand across the sky. I can't believe it.

'So the skipper got through on the radio?'

Charlie nods. 'Left a message at the pub. They should get it.'

After dark we wait on the deck, smoking, looking across to the shore, not knowing, hoping, and then seeing the bright flash of car lights — on, off, on again.

'That's them,' Charlie says, 'C'mon.'

The outboard motor roars and we smack across the black water, churning up strips and specks of green phosphorescence. Charlie holds the rope. We wait for the lights again. 'There they are,' he shouts. 'A bit further north, yeah, that's it.'

It is a strange feeling, skimming fast over the ocean at night, never knowing what is ahead in the dark, waiting for the bang on a rising lump of coral, but it is only a fleeting sensation. It is almost too much to believe that they are really in there, waiting for us, flashing the lights; too big to believe they've got the message and have driven fifty miles, following the coast on a bony red track …

'Slow her down! Slow her down! Getting close.'

I see the pale strip of beach and the line of a little wave breaking onto it and the car lights, higher, shining down on us. We hit the shore and I cut the motor, swing it up, jump out and three shadows cross the sand as they walk down in front of the headlights.

We swing the dinghy side on so it will wash on the edge. Ruth walks right to the water and a rush of coldness comes into me. A wave washes up over her bare feet and the bottom of her jeans.

I hold her and her jumper rises up as she leans on me and I feel her smooth cool skin underneath.

But there is a strangeness between us, too: she has her face against my neck and I know my hair is full of the smell of dried turtle blood and salt water and she has a fine, sweet scent that cuts through everything as we stand together on the soft sand of the beach.

We get a fire going. There is driftwood on the beach and dried snakewood behind the first sandhill and we dig out a little hollow, break some twigs and light them. Jane throws little sticks on top and watches them flare up.

There is probably no one within fifty miles of us tonight, except the fellows on the boat; a long way out near the reef we can see the dull masthead light wink across the water.

The girls have brought wine and chocolates. We watch the fire. Ruth sits near me, her knees up, hands clasped around them. They tell us about the drive, nearly hitting a roo and never really believing they would find us until Ruth spotted the light between a cutting in the sandhills.

The wood in the fire breaks into coals and we sit quietly for a while until Charlie suddenly says, 'We sank the dinghy a couple of days ago. Scared shitless we were!' He laughs.

'What happened?' Claire says. She's been leaning back near him, moving her feet in the sand near the fire, but now she sits up.

Charlie tells them the story. It is nice looking at the fire with Ruth's hand on my leg, feeling how quietly she listens. I put my hand around under her blouse and onto her back. As Charlie speaks, it seems we are all sharing a secret.

We were out near the reef a mile north of the main boat with a heavy load of ten big turtles when we started our run home into a slight southerly chop.

Charlie coiled the harpoon rope and sat on the turtles as we moved heavily through the water. I bailed water and blood as it ran back into the well at the stern, but most of the weight was in the forward half of the dinghy, forcing the bow down.

'Bloody low in the water,' I said, and Charlie moved back near me and the shift lifted the bow slightly and some more water ran down and I bailed it.

We were silent, moving into the low, chopping swells. A bigger swell slopped over the harpoon deck and washed into the dinghy.

'Going to have to ditch a couple of these turtles,' I said. But we didn't do it; we watched the dinghy and the ocean and then, slowly, perfectly, as if we'd already pictured it, the bow did not lift over a swell; it cut through and under and a heavy wash of water flooded in.

'Hang on! Christ!' Charlie said. The bow angled down under the next two swells and I saw a turtle start to float and we were sinking.

The hull tilted away and rolled and I was swimming. The dinghy floated upside-down just under the surface and we hung onto the side, treading water and watching the turtles float away. They were too close to death to be able to swim but some flapped lazily as if coming to life again.

'Grab the bucket! Grab the bucket!' Charlie shouted. It was starting to sink. I reached under and got it.

We hung on, treading water in the spreading blood of turtles.

'We've got to get her back over,' Charlie said. 'Can you get a foot onto the lip under the gunwale?'

'Yeah, got it.'

'Okay, push it down. If we grab the keel it might roll back. You right? Okay. She's coming. Roll, you fuckin' bastard! Steady! No, wait, wait! Okay, let's go again.'

The dinghy rolled and floated upright, full of water. Charlie pulled himself into it and stood up with the bucket. He bailed furiously.

'You have to go like buggery at the start,' he shouted. 'You bail flat out for a couple of minutes; you can get on top of it.'

He thrashed with the bucket while I swam at the side and the gunwales cleared the surface.

'You've got it,' I said. 'The gunwales are clear. Here, have a spell.'

We bailed it dry, untangled the anchor rope and tossed the anchor out again. The bow swung around into the southerly chop.

We'd been sitting there resting for only a minute when the first tiger shark cruised past. It came like a shadow under the turtle blood still spreading in the water. We watched and said nothing, but when it had gone Charlie held his hands on his knees and said, 'Look at that,' and I saw the trembling in his legs. 'Can't stop it.' Mine were the same. He looked at me and said, 'Hey, fuck that for a joke, mate.'

I push a broken piece of burning wood back into the fire. Charlie stretches his legs out and says, 'Got out of the water pretty fast, I can tell you. And then, to top it all off, this bloke gets bitten by a turtle on the way home.' He looks at me and laughs.

'A turtle bit you?' Ruth says.

'Yeah, under the arm.'

'God! How did that happen?'

'Well, we got a couple of turtles back that were floating around. The other dinghy came over and started to tow us back. I was reaching under the bow for my smokes and a turtle grabbed me.'

'Let's see,' she says.

'It's nothing, can't see much. Just a bruise really.'

'It clamped on pretty bloody hard,' Charlie says. 'Had to stick my thumbs in its eyes to get it off. Jesus, it was funny.'

'You shouldn't be cruel to them,' Claire says.

Charlie looks at her. 'Jesus. It was locked onto his armpit. Had to do something.'

'I just don't like the thought of them suffering,' she says, looking at her cupped hand as if studying her fingernails.

I want to make a joke of it so I say, 'Charlie saved me from certain death. I was being eaten by a killer turtle.'

Claire smiles at me over the fire and her face promises everything: a pact is made between us that is full of sad love and distance. When she looks at the fire again the smile stays, as if moving towards warmth is always a graceful turning.

She leans against Charlie. Jane rests her head in his lap.

After a few minutes Charlie stands, holding Jane. She's

asleep. 'I'll put her in the car and get some more wood,' he says.

He walks away towards the low sand dunes and the car and in a couple of minutes is back. 'Nothing much around here, might go for a look up the beach.' He looks down at Claire. 'You coming?'

We watch the two of them walk away along the beach until they merge into the dark.

I pick up the wine bottle. 'You want a bit more of this?'

Ruth holds out her plastic cup and I pour some in.

'Were you scared?' she asks.

'When we sank?'

'Yeah.'

'Things like that happen all the time, well, not sinking, but falling out of dinghies, working in amongst waves. You get used to it.'

We are silent and in the silence I believe she wants me to be strong, brave. I feel she wants something else, too, and I know I have to give it to her. I'd been scared, of course, but it was only after, when we were safe, sitting in the dinghy, and saw the cold length of the shark.

And that was a different fear: it was just like little waves lapping at our safety. I hadn't been scared in the water, but I'd seen the fear on Charlie's face and his frenzy with the bucket. But it had been his wild determined thrashing that had refloated us.

What had frightened me most, I think, was knowing that we'd had the chance to avoid it: there had been a moment, maybe even a full minute, when we could have tossed some turtles out, lightened the load, made it safe, but we didn't. I don't know why. It was a perfect moment for both of us, though, of knowing each other; we were taken out of ourselves and were together in a new place and we'd abandoned our skill, and our courage to get there. Perhaps it was fear. I've always thought that Charlie's fear was easy to see. He took it with him when he went far out into the dark and the deep. I'd seen him; I'd watched him go.

'The fire's going out,' Ruth says.

There is just a low pile of coals now. The moon has come up over the hills. It is white with a ring of blue white light and the beach has changed and is cool and pale. A slice of moonlight slides on the dinghy as it washes below us at the edge of the water.

Ruth says, 'Don't you like talking about it?'

'What? Sinking the boat?'

'Mmmm.'

'Well, that was about all there was really, we put too many turtles into it, too much weight, and down we went.'

She doesn't answer and I can feel the strange and shocking lightness and strength of her shoulder underneath the jumper. A faint breeze blows a small flame across the fire. I get up. 'Where's Charlie with that wood? I'll go and grab some.'

She looks at me, laughs and says, 'I'll stay here.' And then, suddenly, she jumps up, grabs my arm and pulls me down onto the sand with her. She has both her hands at the side of my face, her fingers in my hair and she kisses me. Her face is warm but her back, under the jumper, is cold and smooth. She's too honest for me, I think. I don't know where she belongs or where I can go with her, but her eyes take me quickly to a place she wants us to be in;

it is like the bubble of space I'd shared with Charlie before we sank.

'You smell funny,' she says, and lowers her hands away from my head and moves them down my arms until she holds my hands. She laughs, 'What's that smell?'

'It's turtles, it's oil and blood, the smell of them. Gets right into your bones.' I stand up. 'If I don't get the wood the fire will be out.'

She laughs. 'Better not let the fire go out.'

I walk away and along the beach. Thirty yards from the fire I cross a turtle track. It ripples up from the water's edge in the moonlight towards the low hills. I turn towards the sand dunes and up over the first slope. My feet sink deeper into the soft sand on the other side and there, below me, in a pale hollow at the bottom, are Charlie and Claire, naked, clasped to each other on the blanket. They haven't seen or heard me, they don't move. I can see the dark of her hair where it falls across him. In the moonlight they are peaceful, pale and almost deathly still, but I am sure they aren't asleep, perhaps they are close to sleep, but they haven't fallen away from each other yet, as if, even as they come nearer to dreaming, they are holding close to what they can take with them.

I step back, quietly, and reach the top of the hill again and walk back down to the beach and along it until I see a thick piece of driftwood on the sand.

Ruth is walking back from the car when I put the wood down and she says, 'I went up to see if Jane was okay, she's sound asleep, she looks gorgeous. Did you see the others?'

I break a piece off the end of the wood and look along the beach. 'Don't know when they'll be back.' There are a few dull coals. I push them together and put some more wood on. The fire starts to smoke, so I kneel and blow gently and soon the flames jump up. I've always loved that moment when the flames leap into life.

I feel pretty strange trying to hide it from her. I don't know why I can't say, 'They're up behind the sandhill fucking themselves silly.' Because it isn't true, I suppose. Well, maybe I could try to tell her what I have really seen and what I think is true but I only say, 'Hey, I nearly wrote you a letter the other day.'

She brushes a thick wave of hair away from her forehead. 'Nearly? What do you mean?'

'I was thinking about it, out on the boat.'

She is kneeling on the sand and shuffles towards me, her eyes excited.

'And what did you think about? What did it say?'

'Not much. Turned into a little poem … sometimes it's easier to say things when you write them down, easier than talking, I mean.'

'Do you really think that?'

'For me it's easier.'

'But we talk.'

'Do we?'

'We're talking now, aren't we?'

'Yeah, course.'

'So what's so hard to say?'

'Nothing, really. But don't you think that silence sometimes says more than all the rest?'

She smiles. 'Don't know. Come down here, let's put it to the test.'

She grabs my legs, pulls me down, leaps on me. We laugh and she growls like a cat as we roll together and then I'm on my back, underneath, as she straddles me with her legs, pushes my arms down into the sand and says, 'Got you now.' Her flushed, excited face is inches from mine but she turns suddenly, as if hearing something. I lift my head and see Charlie and Claire walking back towards our little circle of light.

'Oh Christ,' Ruth says.

I sat on the wharf. The wind had dropped. There are times when it drops away at night and then blows from the south-east before dawn. I wasn't cold. It's a funny thing, but sometimes on a cool night if you're sheltered and near sheltered water you can feel warm. That's how it was. The water was still and flat below me. When I looked across at the silent boats and the lights and buildings beyond them, the lights were shining out of the water too.

Fear is another funny thing. A few days after the fire and the girls on the beach, Charlie and I brought a load of turtles back and saw the other dinghy tied up at the stern of the main boat.

'Just get the turtles out,' the skipper says. He's angry. 'Come on, throw a sling up.'

We unload. 'What's wrong with him?' Charlie says to Ernie, when the skipper is out of range.

'It's Martin.'

'What about him?'

'He fell down in the dinghy. Broke his wrist, I think.'

The skipper comes back, sharpening his knife and says to Charlie and me, 'You two get fuelled up and back out there.'

When we're at the fuel drums Ernie says, 'Martin belted himself over the wrist with the gaff, that's what really happened. So he could get off the boat and back to town. Mad bastard.'

'But where is he now?'

'I dropped him at the beach. Skipper got on the radio. Someone's coming out from town for him.'

Later, out in the dinghy, Charlie waves me to stop and I cut the motor and we drift. He lights a smoke. 'Why do you reckon he did it? He could have organised to get to town with two good hands, for Christ's sake.'

'Yeah, I don't know. Maybe he's in the clear this way. I mean, if it's an accident he can come back any time he likes, won't lose any wages.'

'Bullshit,' Charlie says. 'He won't get paid for turtles he doesn't catch.' He pauses. 'I think he wanted to get away from Sarge, he hates his guts.'

'Yeah, maybe.'

We take off to chase another turtle and as we pull it in he says, 'Would you do it?'

'I doubt it. I'd make sure you did it for me.'

He laughs.

Two days later we come around the cape and into the gulf and drop anchor in the early afternoon. The ocean is pearly calm as we cut across it towards the shore, the dinghy making a fast spreading wake.

I can see Martin standing on the beach near the water, his arm in a sling, and then I see Ruth and Claire walking down from the car park with Jane skipping ahead.

I don't get a chance to talk to Martin until later. We're at the pub and when he goes to the bar I follow him.

'Why did you do it?'

He looks at me with his bright searching eyes. 'Just

wanted to get the fuck off the boat for awhile.'

'Is it bad?'

'It's not broken. Big bruise, that's all.'

When I was a kid I had a gidgee with a steel point and rubber sling. One morning I was shooting it into the ground, sticking the barb through bits of leaf and bark. My young brother was standing in my path as I moved forward. Pull. Thud. Pull. Whack. Closer.

'Get out the road. I'm coming that way. I'll just keep shooting. Don't move and you'll get it.'

'Don't have to. My ground as much as yours.'

Pull. Thud. The rubber flopping loose after each shot. The spear driving deep into the ground. The small feet very close.

'Don't shift and I'll get you.'

The quiet face and firm feet. And the spear going down silently into his flesh. Deep. Right to the barb. The sound of his shocked whimpering and then his scream.

'What's wrong?' Martin says.

'Nothing.'

His eyes are on me. He's had a few beers.

'Joe, listen. Sometimes I have to make my own moves and sometimes they're a bit different. Okay?'

'Yeah, it's okay, you mad bugger.'

I take a glass of wine back to the table for Ruth and a jug of beer. It is late afternoon, but still warm in the sun. Charlie and Claire haven't arrived. There are quite a few people I don't know, new faces in town. A woman at a nearby table leans over and asks for my matches. She is about forty, maybe older, and she looks weatherbeaten. So does the man next to her. She looks sad, too.

Ruth is flicking my leg under the table and smiling.

'Who are these people behind us?' I ask. She looks around. 'That's the shearers. They've just finished at one of the stations. Came in last night. Nearly as rough as you fellers.' She laughs. It is good to be with her.

There is music from a jukebox near the wall of the pub and after a while I walk over. I'm standing looking at the selection when the woman from the shearers' table comes and stands alongside me.

'Where you fellers from?' she asks.

'We're turtle fishermen. Just come in for a couple of days to unload the boat.'

Her dress is old-fashioned, ragged and a bit dirty, and she is wearing an old pair of leather sandals. She doesn't say anything for a moment and then grabs my hand and thrusts it up under her shirt onto her breasts and holds it there. We have our backs to the tables.

'You're nice,' she says.

My hand is warm against her and for a little while I don't want to move but then I draw away, take her wrist, hold it for a moment, let go and walk back to the table.

When we leave, Ruth and I watch the shearers and the jukebox lady getting into a ute, laughing. They drive off.

'You coming home?' Ruth asks, leaning on me in the parking area.

'We're unloading in the morning. I'll sleep on the boat. It'll be an early start.'

The next day it is all right and she doesn't seem disappointed about anything. We unload the boat in the morning and then have a few hours to spare. Ruth comes to the beach with us in the afternoon. Charlie is happy. We all are.

We swim and then I sit on the beach with Ruth, watching the others in the water. The ocean is warm and flat and glassy calm. The boat is anchored in the usual place, a few hundred yards from shore. It seems strange, lying on the beach, looking out at it, as if totally abandoned, as if no wild curses and shouts or fresh blood have flowed across the decks; it is like a picture of a grey boat sketched on a piece of pale blue paper.

'Look at her,' Ruth says. 'She loves it.' Jane yelps with excitement, clinging to Charlie's back in the shallows as he romps about like a horse. He makes wild horse noises and Claire, lolling quietly in the water, laughs. I watch Charlie buck Jane high. She splashes down into the deeper water and he scoops her up, both hands under her arms, lifts her high and drops her down.

Claire walks out of the water, brown, her hair sleek, dripping.

'Come on you two, it's beautiful.' She picks up her towel and flicks it playfully. 'Go on, go in.'

'All right, all right,' Ruth says and takes my hand and pulls me. I follow her down and dive and swim out underwater with my eyes open, pulling myself over the sandy bottom. The deeper water is cooler. Ruth says, 'Look at this.' She has her hands cupped together as if she might be holding a small shell, but when I come close she opens them up to show me they are empty, shrugs and splashes the water at me.

We stay until the sun has gone below the hill and the ocean turns a rosy pink. I lie on the beach as she strokes my arm. We lean into each other and kiss and I love it even as I wonder why it is impossible to lose myself to her with Claire sitting just a few feet away talking to Charlie.

Later, on the back step of the house, when we look down over the town, I wonder again why I have to stay so distant from someone who makes me happy.

She is sitting on the step with a glass of wine and says, 'Will you be glad when it's over?'

'What?'

'The season, the turtle fishing.'

'Did you think I would be?'

'Will you be?'

'When it's over?'

'Yeah. What are you going to do? What are we going to do?'

Her legs are tucked up, hands clasped over her brown knees.

'I think Charlie's going to get back on the machines somewhere.'

'I'm not talking about Charlie, what about you?'

I don't really know what to tell her. 'Don't know, see what happens when we get the boat back to the city.'

We sit in silence for a little while. The house is empty. Charlie has gone with Claire and Jane. I don't know where. We are leaving on the boat in the morning for another two weeks.

I lean across, pull her towards me. We go into the house to the bedroom and lie down on the bed. The fan above us swirls slowly, blowing the air around, blowing the stillness and silence away.

I heard a boat start in the darkness, a deep throbbing. I looked out across the harbour to the lights behind the water. A siren faded away down a street.

I had a sudden, warm feeling about what Sonny looks

like, asleep. There was a phone box I'd seen when I crossed the railway track. It was only a hundred metres away. He'd be asleep with Sally on the big bed. It was late, though. What the hell.

I walked down to the phone box, found a couple of dollar coins, swung the door, stepped in and dialled. It rang for quite awhile and then she was there, sleepy.

'Yes. Hello.'

'It's me.'

A moment's silence. 'It's almost one o'clock.'

'Sorry. Were you asleep?'

'No, I was sitting up late with my little flickering lantern doing my diary.'

'Really? And what did you write?'

'Well, no whales to be burnt, but I stitched myself up a fine waistcoat and, oh, yes, Sonny rode off on his pony with Billy, the Aboriginal lad, to check a few cattle on the hills.'

'Is he asleep?'

'Course he is, where are you?'

'Fremantle.'

'What are you doing?'

'Nothing much. I'll be back tomorrow. Today, I mean. Is it really one o'clock?'

'About that.'

'Well, I'll be back tonight then. Late afternoon. Maybe five or six.'

'Is that all you rang for?'

'Are you cranky?'

'What do you ask that stuff for? Even the word sounds a hundred years old.'

There was silence, so I said, 'Anyway I'll be back soon.

Can you survive a few more hours without me?'

'Can you survive a few more hours with yourself?'

'Time will tell. The light's flashing. I've got to go.'

I stepped away from the phonebox and climbed up onto the limestone rocks of the groyne.

From the rocky wall I could see both ways along the dark coast.

I looked at the sea. Little chopping swells slapped and splashed at the boulders below me. The lights of two ships anchored far out were the only bright specks in the darkness. Behind me the city flickered.

In the south the coast disappeared into the dark, but I imagined the shape of it and empty beaches with white lines of breakers and the crumbling cliffs closer to home and then the river; if you followed the river back from the mouth tonight it would be black and smooth and a duck would probably clatter away near the paperbark trees and if you veered away and crossed the paddock and the creek, in twenty minutes you could walk up the last hill to the house and maybe if Sally was still awake there would be a light on in the bedroom window.

Usually when I'm away from home I think of it as a stormy place, wild along the coast; the place where Lizzie's people settled and hacked at the trees to build a hut near a creek and hear at night the strange new cries and sounds of the bush.

I think about men on horses and women: Lizzie and my grandmother and others like them who might have found a clearing in the bush, a special place to go quietly into after the blood of children.

And there are flat rocks along the creek beds, crusty

with dried lichen. The rocks look very old and where the shade falls over them you can sit in the quietness and it's easy to believe that others have sat there before you a long time ago.

When I was a boy an old Aboriginal man, a friend of my father, came to the farmhouse with a horse. He made a movement with his hand and the horse lay down on the grass as if asleep. Then the old man touched it again, gently, and the horse rolled right over and 'slept' on the other side.

I don't know what the old black man and his horse has to do with me or Charlie's death or Lizzie, Claire, Sally or anyone else.

And what would Sally make of it all? You know what she'd think, I tell myself.

The breeze stiffened and I snuggled back in behind a big limestone boulder.

For a minute I thought I might walk back to the hotel and stretch out on the bed, but I was tucked into the rocks, and the washing sounds of the water and the clear stars out above the dark ocean made me stay; made it easy for me to go again and be with them and come home on the last leg of the voyage, together.

When I wake at dawn the fan is whirring and cold and I turn it off and wake Ruth. She gets up and drives me to the beach.

Martin brings the dinghy in to collect me. I ask him about his wrist.

'I'll be right, I'll just take it easy for a while,' he says.

For a week he helps out around the boat but can't do

any heavy lifting. Sarge doesn't like it.

'That prick's a freeloader,' he says to me one afternoon when we are down in the freezer together stacking boxes.

I expect a fight, but nothing happens. They keep clear of each other as much as they can, but we all know it is simmering away.

We fish for another seven weeks; one trip to the islands where we have good catches and two others well south on the west coast. Between trips we have the usual stopovers in town. We stayed a week once, when a dinghy started to split and had to be welded.

The skipper had planned to do one last trip to bump up the final tally of turtles. But the cyclone season is getting close and he changes his mind suddenly and says to us all one night: 'No, fuck it boys, it's not worth it. We'll quit while we're in front. Tomorrow we'll start getting ready for the trip home.'

When the skipper talks about 'home', he means Fremantle, eight hundred miles to the south.

And so, on a sultry morning, we say goodbye at the beach for the last time. There are big storm clouds in the west and the ocean is calm and silvery-grey in the sunlight.

The dinghy is well loaded as we head out to the main boat; there is a lot of gear: kitbags, blankets, shopping, bits and pieces we've all bought for the long trip. It will take about an hour to sort everything out and then we'll pull the dinghies on board and tie them down.

I look back once and can see the three of them on the beach, standing in a little group. Ruth isn't clear any more — they are all too far away now — but the smell of her is still on me, all the warmth and dampness of her, and I can see the sweep of the sandhills behind, the soft slopes white against the dark cloud.

We sail north out of the gulf, swing around the cape and the lighthouse and head south. In the afternoon the wind blows hard and the skipper says: 'That's all we need. Bloody southerlies. Eight hundred miles punching into it.'

After the sunset the swell lifts too and the grey steel bow falls heavily into the troughs and the spray blasts back across the deck and across the two dinghies lashed over the freezer hatch.

For two days we bang and roll south. We call into Geraldton to refuel. It is a short stay. The skipper wants to carry on in case the weather gets worse.

On the fourth morning Sarge is in the galley, holding a pan over the gas flame on the stove, trying to cook himself little pancakes, his knee jammed into the narrow space near the stove to keep steady as the boat rolls.

Ernie, coming off a two-hour wheel watch, climbs down the ladder from the wheelhouse and as he squeezes past he casually picks up half a pancake and pops it into his mouth. He doesn't get a chance to swallow. Sarge swings around, grabs a handful of Ernie's hair and pushes his head down.

I'm on the aft deck and hear a shout and see Sarge, bent over, slamming Ernie's head up and down onto the wooden bench in the galley. I run in. Sarge has his back to me. I lock my arms around his and can feel the strength in him. Ernie slumps onto the bench and I hold on as Sarge forces me backwards and up against the steel doorway. He snorts and twitches like an animal. I fall out through the doorway and down on the deck and, for the first time, we face each other.

I scramble up. There is a gap between us and water from the deck hose washes over my feet as I back right up to the stern gunwale. Sarge is slightly crouched, arms hanging down as if ready to spring, but I am certain he won't: his face has changed. Sarge doesn't really have any friends amongst the crew but he probably thinks he's closer to me than anyone. He isn't my friend, but I don't hate him either, and there have been times during the season when he's been happy to have me around. That is what saves me.

I look past him to Ernie, sitting up now on the bench in the galley, and I feel sick and angry.

'What'd you have a go at him for? Got the wrong bloke didn't you? He stuck up for Martin, that's all. Why did you belt him?'

Sarge doesn't answer and breathes in gasps, through his teeth. I brush past him and kneel down to look at Ernie's face.

'Can you talk?'

He nods. I yell out for the skipper. He comes down from the wheelhouse and says, 'Jesus Christ,' and puts his hand onto Ernie's head, looks into his eyes.

'Come on, let's get him up into the wheelhouse. Joe, get the first aid kit.'

I see Sarge a little while later. He is silent, tense. I walk past him and say, 'You want to know how Ernie is? He's great. Real good. Looking forward to his first night out on the town.'

I feel weak. In the fo'c'sle, Martin and Charlie are on their bunks.

'Skipper wants to see you, Martin.'

'What about?'

I tell them what has happened.

Martin climbs out. He is back in ten minutes.

'What'd he say?' Charlie asks.

'He said that's the end of it. If me or Sarge wants to take it any further he'll sort it out with the rifle.'

'Sarge won't take it any further.'

Martin looks at me, his eyes shining.

'Course he won't, the weak prick.'

Martin doesn't take it any further either. I think the skipper's threat is believed.

Charlie and I talk about it on the last morning, sitting up at the bow on the gunwale, away from all the others, the wind blowing hard across the grey and white ocean. We are only two or three hours away from Fremantle and can see, already, far ahead, the fine grey smudge of Rottnest Island on the horizon.

Charlie picks at the drying edges of a cut on his knee.

'Do you think he feels bad about it?' I ask him.

'Sarge?'

'Yeah.'

He looks up at me.

'I don't know … he took the easy way out, maybe he planned it that way.'

'What do you mean?'

'He knew he could hurt Martin more if he had a crack at Ernie, and that's what he did. I don't think the bastard would be very sorry. Anyway, fuck him, what's the plan for tonight?'

'Have a quiet one?'

'Why not?'

Just on dusk, as the sky fades and lights begin to show the

shape of buildings, we tie up to the fishermen's wharf in Fremantle and Charlie steps up onto the old timbers and says, 'Jesus.'

There is a strange sensation when you feel solid land again after a long time at sea. As we walk he exaggerates a swaying movement and laughs. 'Haven't even had a beer yet.'

Three hours later the swaying is real. The pub is full of music, people, voices, laughter. Charlie asks a girl for a dance. I watch from the bar and catch his eye and he thrusts his arm into the air. It is a wild salute above the swaying bodies and dreamy shining faces.

Later, when the place closes, we are out on the street.

Charlie is drunk, swaying and laughing. He points towards two girls. 'Come on Joey,' he says, 'chat 'em up. You do the talking, you're good at that.' But the girls get into a taxi and we start on the walk back to the wharf.

'Hang on,' Charlie says. 'Hang on, no hurry, gotta have a leak,' and he stands in the street, rocking, relaxed, just the way he would have on the ocean with the boat moving under him.

I see a police car stop. Two policemen grab him.

'He's all right,' I say. 'We're on our way home.'

'He's coming with us.'

'No, no mate, we're going back to the wharf, we're going to sleep on the boat, we're right.'

'You better come too,' the policeman says.

So we go, bundled into the back of a van to the gaol.

The cops are okay. They take our fingerprints.

'You're his mate are you?' one of them asks.

'Yeah.'

'Righto, well you can both cool off in here for the night.

You can't go around pissing in the street you know.'

They take us to separate cells. Mine is tiny, dark and cold. There is a mattress on the concrete floor and a toilet bucket.

'Charlie, where are you?' I call out. There is no answer. I lie down on the mattress. At different times during the night I'm woken by an old man crying out. 'Water, bring me some bloody water.'

I climbed out of my little sheltered space amongst the rocks and walked to the railway track but didn't cross and turned, instead, towards the beach and when I reached it took my shoes off and felt the cool sand. There was an old stone building just above the high-water line and a streetlight near it. The light shone down over the sand to the water.

I followed the beach for a while and then saw another old building I recognised, so I climbed over a little sandy bank and walked towards it. The road was cold on my bare feet. At the first intersection I saw the pub, only fifty metres away on the next corner.

There was no movement. The place was locked. I used my room key to open the side door and went in. A dim night-light showed the outline of the staircase and I walked up and along to my room, opened the door, went in and lay down on the bed.

The room was cold and I pulled a blanket up over myself. The door onto the little balcony was slightly open and the breeze moved the curtain making a small, fuzzy patch of light play across the ceiling. For a moment I was reminded of being in a church. There is a stillness in a church that shrinks away from candle flames. It is different to the stillness of a river early on a cold morning when light comes slowly to shape the water's path, curving the banks high with clean trees rising higher, lighter, until all of the early shade slides away to wait, deep, under the new silver of the moving stream.

But the quiet room shrank further away and a black wind blasted me on the bed and it was the idea of death. I fought and sat up, shaking with the huge coldness of the fact of death in me, the enormous difference. I sat there, not wanting to know. And, slowly, the only truth left in the room came at me: it was like clouds of black smoke rolling across burnt land and I had to shut my eyes tight. I sat right up, shaking, remembering a place I'd been to with Charlie and how we'd seen a whale, far out, and gone to look down where it'd gone down into the deep blue water swirling in shadow, mixed blue-black as if it had drawn up the depths and pulled down the sky. We'd watched the water roll darkly like a dying eye. And now that I'd come close again it was still just as hard to hold him. And the others, too: Lizzie, my father, all of them.

After a while, I don't know how long, I turned the light on over the bed and opened one of the books. There was a very short poem at the front, just a few lines. I read it and then lay back. An idea, or a feeling, began to drift into me.

I felt I was going into a secret place, thirsty, listening, hearing water. I realised it was the world of the little poem which had described a figure, leaning over, reflected in a pool.

I started to see other shapes and colours, trees and shrubs and a circle of blue sky. I saw deep into the pool where the sunlight lit the perfect stillness of twigs resting on the sandy bottom.

The poem made me think about words again and what they can do, what they can do if you say them to someone and what happens if you don't. Simple words, hard and smooth as little stones, easy to hand over, easy to say, 'Here, take these.'

I don't know what time I went to sleep, probably about four in the morning. I woke late, had a shower, packed up my gear and went downstairs. There didn't seem to be anyone around and then I heard some movement behind a door and Col, my straggly-haired drinking mate, came through.

'Hello.'

'Morning,' he said. He was carrying a plastic basket full of bar towels. 'You want to settle the bill? I'll fix it.'

We went to the little office and I paid him.

'On your way now are you?'

'Yep. Heading home.'

'Good luck.'

'Thanks. I'll see you later.'

He nodded with a quick roll of the lips and I picked up my bag and walked out.

I was hungry driving out of the city, hungry and happy. I felt like an old soldier, marching home.

But God you're a bloody idiot, I thought, and started singing like a happy fool and saw a place where I could get a coffee and maybe a toasted sandwich. I pulled over.

The trip home from the city was fast, happy. I wound the windows down and sang into the wind and said a lot of silly things out aloud, with the sun flying until I came into the hills of bush and trees that always make you feel the change; the darker, secret, shady country that leads to the town. It was bringing me in again, bringing me home.

I crossed the bridge over the river, drove through the town, turned off onto the coast road — not far to go now — and up ahead I saw the girl walking, swinging along. She hung one finger out, hitching, and in her other hand twirled a dandelion.

I stopped the car. She wore tight black jeans and a red shirt. I leaned over, opened the door and she got in. Her face was startled, excited. I'd say she was about twenty.

'Where are you heading?'

'Out to the beach.'

'Okay.'

She twirled the flower. 'Look, I just picked this. Back there.'

I glanced at her holding the flower and looking at it.

'You know what?' she said, her eyes bright. 'I'm pregnant. I just found out. You're the first person I've told.' She paused. Her voice and her words rushed and stopped, like someone wildly happy or shocked.

'I just came from the doctor's. I was going to walk all the way to the beach, but I saw you coming and … well.' She shrugged and laughed.

I took her right to the coast and she got out with her big, startled smile, holding the flower, and walked jauntily across the car park, turning to wave as I drove off.

SIX

'Sally,' I said. 'In the morning let's get up early and walk to the river. Just for an hour or two.'

She'd been home only fifteen minutes. I'd made cups of coffee and we were sitting outside the house on the step.

'Aren't you going to tell me about your trip?' she asked.

'I told you.'

She put her cup down on the step. 'I don't know about the river. We're going to Miriam's tomorrow night.'

'What for?'

She looked up quickly. 'You knew about it. I've told you. She's having a little party for one of our staff. Ann's going overseas.'

'We'd be back from the river before lunch. What do you think, Sonny?' He'd come out of the house with a yo-yo, concentrating hard, rolling it up.

'Watch,' he said. 'No, wait.' He rolled again.

'Now, watch this,' and he flicked the yo-yo down and it sprang up into his hand. He looked at both of us, his eyes alight, and flicked it down again.

'Sonny, you want to go to the river tomorrow?'

187

He didn't answer.

'Sonny?'

'All right,' he said.

'You want to?' I asked Sally again.

She looked down the valley below the house, laughed and started to sing, 'Down by the river, I shot my baby …'

'Yeah, okay,' she said. 'We'll go.'

We were late getting away. The sun was well up. Sonny sat at the table with a bowl of breakfast. His yo-yo was in front of him. We didn't rush. I put three oranges and a small water bottle in a plastic bag and walked outside the house to wait. A twenty-eight flew up onto a branch of the peppermint tree. It flicked its head, showing the sharp line of green and yellow and the little blood-red slash above its beak.

After a few minutes I went back into the house to the bedroom. Sally was standing in front of the mirror.

'Won't be a minute,' she said.

In the other room, Sonny had finished his breakfast.

'Come on mate. Just leave the bowl. We'll fix it up later.'

Sally came out. I carried the bag with the oranges and we left the house and walked down the hill towards the creek. Sonny trailed behind us with his yo-yo.

We crossed the creek and followed a long paddock down the valley with steep bush country on the other side. There were 'blackboys' with long, bone-coloured spears sticking up out of the thick thatch. Something about blackboy trees always remind me of emus — maybe it's the way that emu feathers hang down like a rounded skirt with the wind in it.

Big old redgum trees grew on the steep hill. We stopped at one and Sonny shoved a dead stick into a bubble of thick red sap.

We scrambled over flat slabs of granite and had to grab at little bushes to stop sliding. I held Sonny's hand.

'Look, see the paperbark trees?' They were below us on the bank with the smooth river behind them. Branches leaned out over the water.

There were some high rocks near the edge. We went around behind them and down onto rounded boulders.

'Can we go for a swim?' Sonny said. The river looked cold.

'Go on, take him in,' Sally said.

'Are you going in?'

'No way.' She took off her shoes, stretched out a leg and dipped her foot into the water. 'It's freezing.'

'Go on Dad.'

I took my shirt off, stood on the rock, looked at the black water and dived. It was head-splitting cold.

Sonny had his shirt off. 'Come in closer Dad and get me. Can I jump?'

'Yeah, you'll be okay.'

'Will you get me?' He hesitated.

I reached out and he jumped and fell into the water. I grabbed him. His face was shocked, excited.

'Float on your back. Here, give me your legs.'

He stretched out, eyes closed, holding his breath, and floated on his back until his legs started to sink. I held him.

'Look.'

A duck flew up from the bank. We watched as it swept away, low over the water and into the distance where the river curved behind steep hills.

'If you follow the river past that bend it straightens and runs out to the sea.'

He clung to me, not really listening.

'You know the place where we go to the beach,' I said. 'The mouth of the river?'

'Yeah, I know.'

Sally called out, 'What's it like?'

'Beautiful. After a while it's just like a warm bath. Hop in.'

She gave me her 'Don't be crazy' look.

I mucked around and splashed with Sonny, trying not to watch her in case she changed her mind. I could see that she was thinking about it and then I saw her at the edge of the water in her pants and bra and she dived in and came up, mouth open, eyes wide and said, 'Oh God! That's so freezing.'

She climbed out and sat on a sunny rock. There were shadows over the dark water from the paperbark trees on the bank but she leaned back where a bright patch of sunlight lit up the rusty rocks and I swam in, holding Sonny, to join her.

We dried out and warmed up and the sounds slowly surrounded us: birds in the bush, close, far away, different calls, and I heard a rustling in the dry leaves near the rocks; probably a lizard.

Sally sat up. 'Let's head back.'

I called Sonny. He'd climbed out on an overhanging branch and was stripping pieces of bark that were so fine and light they floated slowly to the river and drifted past where we were sitting.

'I'll show you something on the way,' I said.

'What?'

'Wait and see.'

Sonny came to the bank and I peeled him an orange as we followed the river upstream. We came to where the creek entered the river. The gully was steep. We crossed and climbed the hill. I reached the top first and saw the old fence.

Sally arrived with Sonny. There was a section of an old split-rail fence — about forty metres — still standing in the bush. The posts and rails were grey, with lighter patches of flaky, dry lichen.

'This is it.'

'A fence?'

'Yeah. Probably built over a hundred years ago. An Aboriginal lived on this land. Old Sam. He built it. He did fencing for the early settlers. But this was his fence, his bit of land.'

Trees grew close to the fence. Branches hung down over it and, in a few places, the green spiky shoots of young 'blackboys' pushed up against the bottom rail. I leaned against one of the posts. It was solid.

I think old Sam was the father of the man who'd made the horse 'sleep'. Maybe the grandfather. And who was Sam's grandfather, I wondered? And his great-grandfather? And before that? Men who walked the bank of the river. Men with their stories of how the river was made and how the old man who made it was struck down and turned into stone where it runs into the sea. Old Man Rock. Struck down by his daughter with his own magic stick as she escaped with her lover.

I looked at the fence. Old Sam might have put his axe down, I thought, and walked for a minute through the bush and stood watching the river move slowly on towards the sea.

Fences would have meant something else for Lizzie. As

a girl she rode with her father on the coast hills to check the cattle. Later, after she married, fences would have been starting to go up and mark the boundaries of the cleared land. And Lizzie's husband knew all about that, he was a good builder: fences, sheds, stockyards. Maybe he stood outside their hut after she died and thought about building a rail so any stranger riding past could stop, sling the reins over it and shout out, 'Hello, anyone around?' and he could walk out and say, 'Yes. Yes. We're here. Come in, have a cup of tea.'

Or perhaps he just stood there, listening, and then walked back towards the lantern glow and the children, pausing at the door as if held by a familiar sound, so that he had to stretch hard until it broke behind him and frayed back into the night.

My father built fences too. I watched him. And he shot a bull to save his mother. She was Lizzie's sister. The bull belonged to a neighbour and was mad. Put something up and he'd break it down. I was a baby when the bull died. I heard the story later.

The bull had come again in the morning and broken through a fence and rammed the cowshed and my father had watched as it snorted and wheeled in a heavy run between the shed and the old house where my grandmother was hanging washing on a line strung between two fruit trees. She ran, cut off, and crawled under an old cart. The bull stopped and kicked out lumps of dirt, leaned down and struck its horns into the ground. And my grandmother, cowering under the wooden cart, heard the shot and hugged the earth as the bull fell and my father lowered his gun.

'This is probably the oldest fence in the district,' I said. 'He built it pretty well.'

'How old is it?' Sonny asked.

'About a hundred years.'

Sonny climbed onto the bottom rail. 'A hundred!' he said.

'I built fences once,' I said to Sally. 'Just for a while. Before we met. I worked for a bloke building fences.' She nodded.

We walked down through the bush again and up over the next hill until we came to the long valley with the paddock on one side and the bush on the other and we crossed the creek and started up the last hill to the house.

It was getting dark. I sat down to watch the news on TV. I'd been dressed and ready to go for half an hour. Sally was in the bedroom.

I heard a knock on the door and went out. It was the babysitter, a girl about fifteen years old, one of Miriam's kids. She had thick, rusty-coloured hair tied in a pony tail. She followed me and stood in the room while I went off to find Sonny. He came out, fiddling with a clothes peg and a lackey band, trying to make a little gun.

'I'll go and see what Sally's doing,' I said.

She was putting her lipstick on and came out smiling and said, 'Hi Jenny. I'll show you where everything is. Sonny will be tired tonight. We walked to the river today.'

'Is it near here?' Jenny asked.

'Half an hour's walk.'

'It must be nice.'

'It's lovely.'

We drove to town. I stopped at the pub in the main street to buy drinks.

'What do you want?'

'Let's get a bottle of wine. Do you want beer?'

'I'll get a couple,' I said and went into the bottleshop and found the wine she'd like and a few beers for me.

Walking back to the car I saw a couple of the young locals slide down the main street on skateboards and I stopped to watch them swing around the corner at the intersection, leaning into the bend, their bodies flowing and I had the old feeling of wonder about graceful balance ... the mystery of it — as if some magic man, snake charmer, rope dancer or someone like that had held a thick length of rope and made it stand up and sway in the air. The flying riders had shaggy blond hair and before they disappeared I thought: nothing, not a sweet bloody thing could sail so free and loose past the square buildings of our street.

This was our main street, the long hill rising through the town, or falling — whichever way you looked at it — and ever since I was a boy this is where you came to from the farms to see the other people.

Once it had been only a track, muddy in winter, with horses and carts; women probably lifted their skirts to cross and chat to a friend they hadn't seen for a month who'd just tied her horse to a tree on the other side.

It must have been like that; there are old photos and all the stories. And there were times when they left here, later, families moving on. I remember the last drinks in the pub while I mucked around outside with Harry Bell and his brother. Their father's old truck seemed loaded high with the whole world: chooks and ducks in wire cages, mattresses and beds, old boxes, drums, saddles, shovels, a big dark wooden chest, bags that once held potatoes stuffed full of something, buckets, Mrs Bell's sewing machine, an old copper, bits and pieces of a farm thrown on the back in a heap, hanging over the sides, loaded high, and on top two dogs waiting for old man Bell who was in the pub with my father and some of the other local farmers having a farewell drink before heading out of town.

And then out they all came and we stood on the street while Mrs Bell climbed in the front with the red-haired barefoot daughter and the boys scrambled on the back, the dogs barked and down the hill they went, heading off to a place somewhere in the wheatbelt.

I got in the car, put the drinks on the back seat and turned around and drove up past the park and the War Memorial and that's another thing, too, that will always tell you about the moves of people in a little town: when you see the names you might think about them dying a long way from home but also about the day they left, saying goodbye, heading away, young men, excited, off to the city to sign up and sad, too, knowing there would be more work now for their mothers in the mornings, in the milking sheds — taking it all with them tucked deep down in their kitbags and years later coming home again, some of them, still feeling the shaky ground as they hugged it, back there, way back — hearing a scream turn into silence. They come home to the house where the children had waited in winter nights, under blankets, thinking only of an older brother leaning down and saying, 'C'mon' and being slung up behind him onto the bare back of the horse and hugging around his belly, tight, as he kicked the horse into a canter across the paddock to round up the cows.

Last night, when Sonny wanted a story, there he was: rug pulled up to his teeth in the scary parts but wanting more, saying, 'And what happened to the penguin?' because I'd made two penguins travellers in a circus and one of them was always scared of the cranky lion tamer who said, 'You penguins better do what I tell you. Anyone comes to this circus and thinks they got some special fancy act that's bigger than mine they gotta remember I make the rules,' because the crowds were getting to love the penguins and their playful tricks and the lion tamer was jealous and angry and he shouted, 'You do what I tell you or you'll go in the cage with the lions.'

Sonny pulled the blanket even higher and his startled eyes were turning sad so I said, 'But one of the penguins had a plan and he said to the lion tamer, 'We could do our tricks with you and the lions and then everyone would be happy,' so they did; the penguins rode the lions around the ring and all the people cheered and even the lion tamer loved it and he wasn't angry any more.'

Sonny lowered the blanket and I could see his whole face, almost happy, so I kissed him and said, 'Goodnight.'

We turned into Miriam's street and I parked the car outside her house.

The front door was open. We went in. There was quite a crowd, spread in groups through the house and out to the backyard. We walked in. Miriam saw us; she'd just put a bowl down onto a table out the back and she came to us and said, 'Oh good, you're here.'

'Are we late?'

'No, no, of course not. It just seems to be one of those nights. It's beautiful isn't it? And people came early. They're all just in the mood. Here. Come on. Put those in the fridge. I'll get some glasses.'

She went with Sally to organise glasses and I opened one of the beers and went out to the garden area. Stan, a fellow I'd met a couple of times before, stood next to a table with plates of chips, cheese, olives, nuts, sprigs of celery and little bowls of dip.

'How you doing?' I said.

He leaned over and dipped a piece of celery into a bowl.

'Yeah … can't complain. How about you? Still washing dishes?'

'Non-stop. Washing. Ironing. Mending. I'm pretty slick with a vase of flowers, too.'

Women asked this question in a different way: they'd move in gently and study your answer with a hard fascination, as if they were watching a strange creature wake and slowly unfold. It was like being in a close, slow dance and I loved to perform in the spotlight of their gaze.

'You having something to eat?' Stan asked, moving backwards on the brick paving and sidestepping a hanging basket of ferns.

'I'll sort something out,' I said and took a biscuit and some cheese and went back into the house.

The place was modern and open plan with new furniture. I saw Sally with Miriam, looking at a kind of Japanese curtain, a bamboo frame with rice paper. She waved me over.

'Do you like this?'

'I'm in love with it,' I said. 'What does it do?'

'You can fold it, it's just handy. And you can move it around.'

She looked at me.

'It makes a place look nice, that's what it does.' And she shrugged her elbow into me in a playful way and smiled.

I spent the next hour drifting around. It was a casual atmosphere and people were on the move, wandering from little group to group, from the food table to the fridge and out to the back garden. I lingered in the back yard with the smokers. The easy mood seemed to flow through the place like a breeze.

I talked for a while with Ann, who worked with Sally and was leaving to go travelling, but when she glided away to join her friend I went inside to get a beer. I could hear Sally's voice. She was in a small group standing close and chatting, but out of sight. There was a partition and archway in the wall at the side of the fridge. They were in the next room, just around the corner.

I opened my beer and made out I was studying a couple of photos stuck to the fridge door with little bright magnets. I could hear the careless bursts of laughter, the happy, teasing questions, the reckless replies and gasps of mock horror. If I'd shuffled a couple of steps to the right they might have seen me and waved me to join them. But it was exciting staying where I was; it was like standing unseen as a merry-go-round whirls, hearing the laughs and shrieks — if I'd tried to climb aboard, the whole thing would probably have tipped off balance so I slunk in the bright light, while scraps of laughter and talk landed around me.

I fiddled with my beer can and looked at the photos. One was of two schoolgirls in uniform — Jenny, our babysitter, caught in a clowning pose with a friend. The other picture showed a woman I didn't know holding a baby in her arms.

I heard Sally say, 'He's not like that really, he's more impulsive,' and I concentrated on listening but Stan, coming in from outside, nudged me and said, 'Can I get in there mate?' and I moved aside as he opened the fridge.

We went outside together and I lit a cigarette. Stan didn't smoke.

'Used to, once,' he said, 'not any more.'

There was a change in the noise from inside the house and I looked and saw Miriam tapping a glass jug with a spoon. We went in. She stood, holding the jug, waiting, and then said, 'Now, where is she? Ann. Come on. This is your moment in the spotlight. No escape!'

Ann walked over, holding her wine glass.

'We all wanted,' Miriam began, and then she tapped the jug again, 'Ssshh, come on … Yes, we all wanted to show Ann how much we enjoyed working with her, she's been good fun to have around, lots of laughs, heaps of energy, she's bright and bubbly and I think she's going to have a hell of a time keeping all the Romeos away as she swans around France and Italy, anyway, I'm sure she'll manage.'

She turned to her, 'Ann, it's been great and we all wish you happy travelling and here's a little something for your trip.'

Ann took the present. She looked at it and then around the room.

'Oh ... I don't know ... what do I say? It's been a terrific job. Thanks to everyone, all the girls and Sally for always encouraging me and, well ... just thanks, and I'll send you postcards ... and I'll miss you.' She held the present and Miriam leaned towards her and they hugged.

I watched Ann with her friends around her as she opened the present. Their faces were shining. And then I saw Catherine. It was a surprise, but there she was at the back of the room and she looked the same. I'd known her a few years before. She didn't seem to be with anyone, but this might have been because of the way she looked slowly around the room, letting her eyes rest on something for a little while and lifting her drink in the languid way she'd always had.

We'd met during one of the local theatre productions. She'd played the main character. I'd heard she'd split up with her husband. She was about my age, I suppose, and someone I'd always loved being with and talking to. There was a stillness about her, an intent way of listening. Everything in her seemed to rise and reach out from a lake of calmness.

I watched her. When the group and the talk started to break up she walked out through a side door onto the verandah. After a while I followed and saw her, smoking. I didn't know she smoked. She had her back to me near a hanging basket and was lifting a trailing fern on two fingers, studying the thin, fine pattern.

'Hello.'

She turned, not hurrying or dropping the fern, but lowering her hand gently until it hung down again below the basket and with the same rhythm of movement she reached over and held me to her in a quiet hug.

There was a wooden bench seat near us and we both sat down.

'What have you been doing? You don't live down here any more do you?'

'No. Haven't lived here for two years. I'm in the city. But I try and get down. I bought a little business up there. A craft shop. I get some of my stuff from down here,' and then, assuming a slightly aristocratic accent, she went on, 'Some of my clients are down here Joe, so I'm in town for a couple of days mixing business with pleasure.'

'What happened with you and Brett?'

'Oh! Do you really want to know?'

I didn't answer.

In her quiet, unruffled way she smoothed her skirt with the back of her hand and laughed.

'Well, we just did what everyone else seems to be doing, we broke up.'

She laughed again and I waited and she said, 'Oh, I don't know, I don't know if Brett ever really saw me.'

'Did you show him?'

She smiled; there was a warm feeling between us.

'What I mean is, it was hard for him to see me, he was seeing someone else.'

'Another woman?'

She laughed again, 'Yes ... well, not really, he was seeing another woman in me.'

She thought it was funny and prodded her finger into my arm, smiled and said, 'Maybe you and Brett have something in common.'

She was joking. She reminded me of what Claire might have become.

'But don't talk about me, what about you? What are you doing?'

'Not much.' I wanted to tell her about the writing. She waited.

'Are you reading much?' I asked. I knew she loved reading.

'Hmmm … not enough. Well, I am,' she said. 'I'm doing some study; a couple of units in Aboriginal history and culture. Aboriginal women, really.'

'The early days?'

She nodded. 'All of that … the settlement times, and the role white women played, too.'

'My great-aunt Lizzie wrote a diary,' I said, 'And there's a bit in it about a young white woman who kills her baby. There was some sort of trial. I think Lizzie wrote, "She was acquitted on the charge of murder, a most horrid affair."'

Catherine's hand touched my knee, lightly, as she listened. It was as if she didn't know it was there as she waited for me to go on.

'It would have been strange,' I said, 'For a white woman to have a black man's child, I mean. I think it was usually the other away around.'

The music and noise came at us through the door and open windows as we sat on the bench. She wanted to know all about it — the diary and Lizzie, what she was like and how she lived, and I spent a few minutes telling her. The way she was listening made me want to tell her what I could and when I was finished she was silent for a minute and then said, 'But you haven't told me about you. What are you doing?'

'Not a lot.'

She waited.

'I'm doing some writing.'

There was just the slightest movement of her hand against my leg before she lifted it to brush the hair on her forehead, gently, slowly.

'Well? Come on,' she said.

'Oh, I don't know … whether it's much, I mean. Just people, relationships, that sort of stuff.'

But you do know, I was telling myself. You want to tell Charlie's story and your own. You know you want to say what's important. And you know that figuring out how to do it properly is important. Not hiding anything. Making it all clear. And telling about a long day with Charlie and what it was like afterwards with all the cuts on your hands and being absolutely stuffed, knowing you'd both gone right to the edge of what you could do.

'I wanted to tell about how good it is sometimes with people,' I said.

'Well tell it to me,' she said.

'I'm trying to work it out. Just trying to make it a good story.'

And you want to make it happy, don't you? And try to show what made you follow it. So why can't you tell her that? Because you don't know yet what it was that made you feel as if things had gone cold. And maybe they haven't and even if they had, who wants to tell about something like that? No one. Because you might find there was nothing worth telling anyway. Better just to remember how it was with your father on the horse, bareback, his arm loose around you holding the rein, your legs hanging, rubbing on the horse's sweat, riding down the hill towards the creek, with nothing ever coming to break the perfect rhythm because if it did you would lose the way the sky looked and the mist above the dark trees down along the creek, and the strength of your father's arm across you; you'd lose whatever you always lived for with Sally … but if you can't see what it is, if it is only a strange, numb feeling and you don't know where it's from or what it wants … well, beat it down, beat it back.

'Well, I wanted to write about the strength of people, how they deal with things.'

I could have kissed her for listening the way she was, as if she knew what you said didn't really matter, as if she knew it was the thing behind what you were trying to say that she was hearing, like sometimes when there is the low rush and roar of a winter creek in the distance, hidden a long way in, deep below the hill and trees and you know how it will look. But I wished I could tell her about it simply and clearly, about what everything meant to me: Charlie and Claire, Sally and Lizzie, everyone.

She was waiting in the silences.

'And a story about how you reach down when someone has fallen and you both come together, laughing.'

Catherine looked down at her hands and smiled. I held the cigarette packet out to her and laughed. She took one and I lit hers and mine and looked away and saw Sally, standing under a light on the verandah wall, talking to another woman. Her face was alight and she was smiling, talking, laughing. Everything about her was shining and happy and strong and the light seemed to run along her arm as she laughed and reached out to touch the other woman's shoulder.

For a moment I felt like a child whose eyes shift suddenly, startled away from the dreamy stroking of a mother's hand and the blurry world of sleep by the cry of a bird outside in the night, a cry that wakes a little thrill of shining wings moving under the moon.

I had to go. There was Sonny to get home to. He'd probably be asleep now, dreaming, peaceful. And only yesterday he'd said to me, 'What do you reckon would hurt more? Getting bitten by a bull ant or dying?'

'Getting bitten by a bull ant.'

'So do I, 'cos when you're dead you wouldn't feel anything.'

I stood up and said, 'I'd better round up Sally, we've got the little bloke at home.'

She squeezed my hand and smiled. I left her and walked over to Sally and raised my eyebrows as if to say, 'Are you ready to go?'

She said, 'Do you want to go?'

'No ... when you're ready.'

I walked outside to the car and waited for ten minutes, watching the house, listening to the voices and laughter, and then I went in again and Sally said, 'Oh, you're there, just come and say goodbye to Miriam.'

Driving home, I said, 'What about the babysitter?'

'I'll ring a taxi when we get home.'

After the taxi had come and gone I went into Sonny's room and leaned over the bed, listening to his quiet breathing. When I came out Sally was lying on the couch.

I made two coffees, gave her one and said, 'Catherine is doing some Aboriginal studies.'

She sipped her coffee and looked at me over the cup. 'I don't know if I like everyone jumping on the Aboriginals' case.'

'We did.'

'But we didn't stay on it.'

'But we could have.'

'But we didn't. Because you don't stay on anything. That's what all this is, I think. You can never settle. You never know what you want.'

'But we did want to know more about them, we just didn't do it.'

'Why do you always think there's more to everything?'

'There's more to you.'

'See! You want to joke about it. You're either joking or out of control. Can't you find some sort of middle ground? You told me once that when someone's saying something they really believe in, you should really listen. Well that's what I'm doing now. So why joke about it? Just face the truth of what's in front of you. And I'm sure that's half the problem, too, of going back into the past and raking up a story out of cold ashes.'

Well, maybe she was right. I don't know what I wanted from the past, or the dead. I didn't want to bring them to life. No. It wasn't that. But they had shown me something and perhaps I just wanted to sit down with Sally now and see what it was. Listen for it, together. Hear our own hearts. It seemed so easy, just a simple decision, like saying, 'Let's sit down here for a while and listen.'

I looked over at her. She was waiting. I wanted to see it all clearly with her so I could move on and be like a man who digs a post hole and throws the shovel aside, shoulders the splintering post into position, sweats in the sunshine or shakes the rain away as he rams the earth back into the hole. And maybe she'd push a wet grey branch aside and see me again. Because that's what she wants. It is in her blood to want it. Handed down, woman to woman. Wanting only a man who is close to a threshold of pain that is as common as sunrise to them. And that, I suppose, is what I'd always loved. Well, perhaps you always love what you can only imagine.

'You know,' I said, feeling I needed to say something, 'The other night when the little bloke came into the bed I woke up and got up and you were asleep on the bed with him and it seemed strange, for a moment, thinking about a family asleep — how they've been tossed together, I mean — because when you sleep, there are just all the legs and arms all over the bed, just lying still, like driftwood on a beach; have you ever thought that? How funny it seems to be tossed together like that?'

She put the cup down, looked at her nails for a moment and said, 'When you say something like that, are you really serious or is it just a jokey thing? You know, like something a bit funny that we can't do anything about and doesn't make a difference anyway.'

'Well, I don't know about a joke,' I said. 'It's just a thing that happens, and you're right, there's nothing we can do about it. We wouldn't want to do anything that could change it would we?'

Sally didn't answer, so I went on.

'What do you think you can leave for them?'

She looked up, not quite understanding.

'For kids I mean.'

'What can who leave them?'

'Us ... anyone ... a parent.'

She shook her head and said, 'I know I keep saying it, but why do you worry about all of this?'

'I don't.'

'You do, and you want me to say something crazy like

"Leave them the idea that the stars are warm, bright, warm stars," that's what you want, isn't it? Sure, that's what they need to know; I'll work on it tomorrow, start a campaign.'

She drank her coffee. We were both quiet for a little while. It's a quiet house when no one speaks. You can hear the clock tick.

I glanced at her and she looked up at the same moment and said, 'What's happening with your story?'

'Have you been reading it?'

'No, I don't want to read it, I've got my own story to do.'

'How do you mean?'

'You know what I think, you just have to live it, do things, go forward, make your own way.'

'But who do you do it for? Yourself or others? I mean, you can't really go forward alone, not if you're together at the start.'

'Who's together at the start?' Sally asked.

'All of us. We all are.'

'Are we?'

For a little while I'd thought that our mood would lead into a night of easy discovery, but now, again, I was cold with the idea of failure: somewhere, close, there must be a switch that needed only a gentle flick to light a stage and have us both dancing … seeing each other simply and shining with our simple moves; that is the thing we'd shared at the beginning, the excitement of not looking too far or too deep. To reach out and find the switch now, seemed, for a moment, as if it could be such a simple thing and so easy, just a tiny, innocent act.

I'd been looking at my hands, thinking.

'Well, I don't know,' I said. 'But when we go forward together we step over into a place we both understand, but we bring everything with us, too. We can't leave anything behind. We're loaded up.'

'Why don't you say things clearly? Why do you get into all this obscure stuff about stepping over imaginary boundaries and carrying heavy loads?'

Sally needed an answer and so did I. She waited, but not for long.

'What are you saying?' she asked. 'What is it you really want to do? Am I the problem or is it your own problem? What?'

She shifted on the couch, stretched out, kicked off her shoes and crossed her legs and we both watched her foot drawing circles in the air. Sally has beautiful legs.

I wanted to toss one good, simple comment we could recognise instantly and together, and laugh at ourselves, like coming down on a card in a game of Snap.

It was a long time since we'd gone this far together: it was like being on the shore watching the shifts of light in water and sky; there was time now, surely, to see how the changes moved at our own pace, like the ocean when it breathes ... when it lifts and sighs ...

Sally waited. I wanted to go with her tonight, anywhere ... only together. There was no problem.

'There's no problem,' I said. 'It's not you, me ... it's nothing.'

I wanted the night to linger and last. I tried to make a joke. 'Don't worry Sir, I do him this way!' When we'd lived in the North, teaching the Aboriginal kids, there was a boy, Johnny, and whenever I tried to show him something he'd say, 'I do him this way, I do him my way Sir!'

Sally sat up. 'Remember how good they were at taking people off? A couple of the girls took off the Queen one day — real plums in their mouths — it was like, "I say, this is a most awful place. It's so terribly hot and what on earth can we do about these beastly flies?" It was just hilarious.'

Yes, I could remember. I could remember going across to the building Sally taught in and seeing her outside it on the worn, dry grass with a group of girls, all sitting down, busy, and Sally so white amongst them and one of the girls would look up at me and say, 'Sir, Sir, look what Miss doing!' and I'd sit down with them near the little fire and watch as they took a shiny red and black seed from a small pile, heated a thin piece of wire and poked it through the seed to make a tiny hole; they'd thread the seeds onto fishing line. 'We make beads, Sir, necklace. See? Look at Miss.'

And in the late afternoon we'd sit outside on the verandah of the house, drink a beer or a glass of wine, look across the yellow plains stretching to the hills on one side and the faint line on the other, which was the trees, far away, lining the river and Sally would say, 'What can I teach them tomorrow?' and 'Do you think we can ever teach them anything?' We'd laugh, together, both understanding.

One night we were invited to a corroboree on a flat circle of worn ground near the river. We'd driven for half an hour and it was almost dark when we arrived. The moon came up. Kids ran laughing up the riverbank to the clearing. Hundreds of people had gathered.

When the dancing started I looked around at the people sitting on the ground. A big light had been set up and I could hear, faintly, the sound of a generator. Dust hung over the clearing as the dancers stamped and listened; they were like hunters, stalking, watching, closing in.

In the crowd I saw some of the boys from the school and Johnny, the lanky fourteen-year-old who, only a few day earlier, had draped his arm over my shoulder and said, 'We can tell stories today, Sir?' I could see the stillness of his body and his intense expression telling how he understood the story of the dance.

Sally and I had watched. Ours were the only white faces.

I turned to her now. 'Do you remember the corroboree?'

'Course. I remember the old lady on the river bank who'd caught the big fish.'

It was so good, both of us in this mood. I wanted to say to her, 'You were good, you were happy teaching those girls. They loved you, they were always touching you, smiling, saying, "Look Miss!"'

Sally moved her legs on the couch and said, 'Do you think you only remember the good things?'

'Me?'

'Yeah.'

'Probably.'

'Then why do you drag up all the dark stuff?'

'Dark?'

'Well, maybe you're not dragging it up, but you've slid into it. That's where you are. Moody, serious, like your story.'

She had stretched out again, relaxed, despite what she was saying, with her hand gently pulling at bits of hair.

She'd always done that, at certain times, and now it took me back to when we'd first met and gone into the city and danced and come out later, flushed in the cool night. I remembered her moist skin and warmth and waiting to cross the street with snatches of talk, like, 'Hey, where are we going?' and, 'Just come on, come on,' laughing, taking her hand, pulled together by excitement that was all around us in the city lights, in the night, in each other. I loved to take her hand, pulling, and see how she loved it. And later, in the quiet, when everything had become still, she'd tug at her hair and say, 'Your hands are so rough.' They were rough then, when we met. Not now.

The tap over the sink dripped. I walked over and turned it off.

'Do you really think I'm serious? Too serious?' I asked her.

'A lot of the time.'

'Are you serious?'

She smiled. 'I don't know … but you are, and remember what you always said: "The one thing we've got in common is that we don't take things seriously." Remember saying that?'

I got up from the chair again. 'I'm going to have another coffee, do you want one?'

'All right,' she said. 'But do you remember it?'

'I do, yeah.'

'Well?'

I switched the kettle on, put coffee in the cups. Maybe she's right. I was so close to saying: 'I'm not serious now, only excited. I want us both to go out in the night, I want to hold your face in pale light and walk with you into the dark.' But I didn't say it, of course, because it would have destroyed what I was trying to do; Sally would have seen it as weak. And that might have made her recoil and stiffen into silence. We were moving now, we were going somewhere together. I had to step gently, guiding us around rocks, holding her to me when she shivered. Because it might get cold if we went down near water.

I walked back with the coffee and Sally reached for it, saying, 'So, if you remember, if it was such an important thing for you, why do you seem to have forgotten? I mean, what about the other night? I said something, some little thing, and what happened? You got serious about it. Did you put that in your story? All the charming details, did they go in? You see, you go off on this big trip to hunt down the truth, but half of it you don't even face up to yourself.'

She was right. There had been a fight, but later it had seemed like nothing to me. Except for Sonny. I remember him coming out. The shouting must have woken him and we didn't know. I saw him standing in the doorway, quietly crying, and I took him back to his room.

I didn't know what to say to Sally now. There was a dead tree I must cut up for firewood tomorrow. I'll have to do it tomorrow, I thought.

'It's pretty late,' I said. 'I might go to bed and read for a while.'

She didn't answer and I took my cup over to the sink, walked outside the house and stood there for a little while listening to the rushing, whispering sound the wind made in the trees.

We could pick it all up again tomorrow. There was a long way to go. We'd made a start.

I wanted to take her and go out there together. Meet them all again.

SEVEN

In the morning Sally went to work. She took Sonny in the car to drop him at school. I got the axe and walked out into the bush and found the dead jarrah tree lying on the ground. It had been there a long time, probably ringbarked by my father before I was born, or maybe even my grandfather.

I swung the axe and stuck it in the wood and then sat down on the log. I just wanted to sit there for a while in the bush with the broken shadows and sunlight on the ground. The log was smooth, grey and blackened in patches. A fire must have got at it years ago.

I stood up and swung the axe down and split a chunk off. The wood was a soft pink colour. I hadn't chopped wood for a while and it felt good to be chopping in the sunlight and warmth of the morning. It was early to be getting firewood but this year I'd be ready. Usually, when the winter rains came and swept along the valley, I'd be out in the dark, scraping around for bits and pieces.

I took my shirt off and started chopping again. There were some deep cracks running along the log and I swung the axe into them, splitting chunks off.

After a while I slowed down and moved into a steady

rhythm. I knocked strips off with the back of the axe and chopped them into pieces that would fit the fireplace. It was good to be into the old, swinging rhythm.

I never knew anyone who could chop wood like my father. He would tackle any twisted old piece of bush wood and split it to size. Beautiful swing. Charlie was good with an axe, too. He brought it down with a swinging smack as the boat rolled. He cracked the blade down through the shell of turtles with bits of shell flying and blots of blood in his gold hair.

I want to say, now, why I'm telling about the chopping: I'd been thinking about what Sally said and whether you could really go anywhere alone and after she'd gone with Sonny and I was alone in the house I went out with the axe to chop, not knowing why, not knowing what it means to tell about it in the story. I only knew, walking into the bush, that I wanted to work and break down the log.

So I chopped all morning until the sun came brighter through a space between the crowns of the trees. The axe handle shone smooth. I spat on my hands and swung. Ants came out of the log when I split into their secret home. I knocked and cracked and broke the wood until there were chunks and chips all around on the ground, and then I sat down on what was left of the log. It took a little while before the echo of the chopping drifted away and the light in the clearing became sharper in the silence on the pink wood and the smooth swaying leaves of the trees.

Charlie? Do you remember how we put down our bloody axes and sat on the gunwales, with the gentle lift and fall of the boat? And Lizzie, you've rested in silence. What would you have said? What would you have written? If I had a diary I could say: *Went out into the bush today to get firewood. Chopped a good amount in the morning, then cleaned up the house a bit.*

Or I could organise an afternoon for old friends. We could work together and then sit in the clearing and have some lunch. Would you come, Lizzie? Would you come with your long, heavy dress? I'll ask a crowd, well, a handful anyway. Charlie will be there, you'd like him, Lizzie, with his funny sayings and ropey hair. And my father. You looked after his mother, remember? You were the oldest and she was your little sister. My father will drink a beer with me and Charlie. What will you drink, Lizzie? We could boil a billy. Charlie can light a little fire, any of us could manage that, of course, but watch the way he does it, reckless, fast, squatting down saying, 'Let's kick a bit of heat into this little feller,' because Charlie had his own way with words, made jokes ... and Sally is right: I've painted him dark, but he was funny.

Have I made you dark? I don't think so. Do you really want tea? Would you kick your shoes off to warm your feet at Charlie's fire and swig something a bit stronger? Will you stay the night? Did you bring your lantern and your diary? Here, sit on the log, Lizzie, near the fire. You look tired. And your hair has fallen down. I'll tuck it back. You can rest now. We're all here. This is Ruth. Yes, she's come. And Claire; she is like you.

Lizzie, I see in you what you want me to know: whatever I find here is only a small thing and all the rest is further on. But I'll show you something. We'll have to walk through this bit of bush. Come on. It's not far. Yes, leave the others. Charlie's there. He'll keep them amused. We won't be long. Now, you see? Over there, past the valley? On the other side, on the hill? You see it? That's the old dairy. That's where your little sister came to live and work and die. Yes, my grandmother. When I was a kid my father milked the cows over there. I'd run across the hill and down through the creek and up again to find him in the shed.

But you look tired, Lizzie. Come back to the fire and rest. You're tired and sad and beautiful. Can I talk to you like this? You don't mind? All right. Here they are. Stay here now. Stay with my father. He has plenty of stories. And stay with Charlie and Claire and Ruth. I'll be back. Maybe I'll bring Sally and Sonny. We can sit around the fire and talk.

I walked back towards the house with the axe. Holy Christ, I thought, this business has gone too far. If you want to work, for Christ's sake work. If that's what you're after, get stuck into it.

You can't go jolting back to this all the time. It's like rock hopping. Stand still. Stand on rock. Feel it under you. Look around. You've stood on rock before. Remember? You looked up and Charlie lowered the rope until your feet were planted against the red cliff. Way down below the dozers were pushing through the valley, clearing the way for the railway line. And above, Charlie was leaning over the edge with all of the blue sky behind him. Start her up Charlie! I'm ready to drill this fuckin' rock! I'm ready to ram this steel bit into a crevice so the chips fly like shrapnel!

I went into the house and made a sandwich and thought about going out with the ute, loading the wood and bringing it back, but decided not to. In a couple of hours Sally would be home.

Through the window the sunshine was bright on the grass and the leaves of the trees. I thought about how the ocean would look and the idea of jumping into it made me walk out, get in the ute and start it up. I wanted the clean, cool feeling of water.

On the drive out from the house along the dirt track I looked across at the bush. The chopped log was further in, out of sight; I'd get in there later and throw it on, probably be a good ute-load.

When I pulled up at the parking area there was only one other car. A man was standing on Old Man Rock, fishing.

The offshore breeze had dropped and hadn't swung into the south-west yet. The sea was lightly ruffled closer to shore, but further out long calm strips, like runways, made a patchwork of smooth blue against the darker water. A wave peeled across the bay, pushing white water over the green.

I looked across at the beach and the sand bar blocking the quiet river and further on to the hills with their dark coast scrub and scoops of white where the wind, or maybe the steepness, had made the sand fall smoothly. There was a hawk above the hills, its wings fluttering and then still before it dropped. Sunlight shone on the white beach but the hills had patches of shade falling away from steep slopes. The light on the hills seemed to hover above the scrub like yellow dust. At the far point of the shore the reef lay calm and rusty under light green water.

The river split the valley with shade on the still water where it cut back, away into the hills; wide and silvery dark near the blocked mouth and blacker as it narrowed upstream.

Could I ever look at this beach without thinking of Lizzie and the whale and the fires at night or the Dreamtime story of the Aboriginal girl turning her father into Old Man Rock?

Could I ever see it without seeing myself as a young boy while my father stood on the shore, water washing around his knees, holding the old handline and stumbling sideways and backwards, the line tight, his pants wet, until he was near me, bent over, pulling the line in low and further in, his face grim, not wanting to smile yet until there it was, hard, blue-silver, shining on the sand, out of the water, and gone again with another wave washing up and then silver wet, closer, nearer, jack-knifing into the air, almost on us, safe on the dry sand with my father laughing, standing above the fish, looking at me?

Could I look at the beach without any of that, I wondered. Would you want to, I asked myself, and got out of the ute, walked down, threw my shirt near a rock, ran to the ocean and dived in.

I swam a little way and rested, letting the rip glide me out around a patch of weed I could see under the water and then over clear sand and I swam again towards the first swell and went over it and saw another one ahead, breaking. I dived down and held the sandy bottom and watched the shadowy roll of bubbles pass over me. I came up, out of breath and floated for a moment, resting, and then swam further out.

There was a lull. I looked out to sea and saw the dark line of another swell. I swam to where it would break and rose up in the green lifting water and pulled and kicked into it until I could feel the rush forward and down; I was pushed out in front of the white water and lifted my head as the wave took me fast, fading halfway to shore so I kicked to stay in front, sliding down the clean face until it peaked again and the white water caught me and I raced with it, seeing the beach getting closer, coming in fast to sprawl up the shore.

I walked out, getting my breath back, watching the ocean. The man was still fishing, standing on Old Man Rock. I went back, picked up my shirt and wandered over to him.

'Getting any?'

'Couple,' he said. He reeled his line in and crouched on the rock, baiting the hook. I waited until he flicked the rod and the line sailed out.

'What sort?'

He turned. 'Couple of herring, that's all.'

He concentrated on the rod, fingering the reel.

'Good luck, see you later,' I said.

He looked over his shoulder and nodded.

I want to say something now which I think might blow the smoke away from the trail I've been trying to follow. There is someone ahead — I think it is Ruth, or perhaps it is Claire — but she folds and floats; I have to go on to see her clearly; I'm close, and like you, I started this journey not really knowing where it would take me, only believing that when the scent is strong I must follow it. Well, the scent is strong again and the strange thing is, it is Sally who has turned my head towards it: last night I lay in bed reading and when she finally came in she said, 'Did Sonny go back to sleep?'

I nodded and she got into bed and after a little while of silence she asked, 'Whatever happened to the famous Ruth, anyway?'

My first thought was that she really had been reading my story, but I didn't say anything and then later, after I turned out the light, I realised that Sally probably knew more about what happened to Ruth and me than I did, and she was only trying to help me to see it.

I had the feeling, too, that I was being drawn up into the lifting water of a wave before it breaks, and needed only to strike out, push off ... there is a moment with every wave for a decision: to go with it or to duck underneath; Sally had given me a gentle push, almost like saying, 'Go on, that way now, you're almost there.' And perhaps she's always been at my shoulder and it makes me wonder, now, about the whole business of the 'heavy heart' thing. Was it ever really there? I don't feel it now. Was it all imaginary? No ... I have to be honest, there was something and before I go on I'll put it down here. It was real. I know, because of a few lines I scrawled down one day not long before I started to tell this story. I wrote this about a week, or maybe two, before Charlie's 'visit', before he came to trigger the whole journey. So here we go, these are the words: I've found them, I even jotted a date at the top (it was two weeks before Charlie 'came').

The world is still while Sally sleeps. The sun has gone away and the birds wait without sound. A heartbeat will start the red sun moving and make the river run and shake the colours on water, rock and leaf while Sally sleeps. But I can make a cake and we can drink tea and let the laugh of a child reach us and raise our eyes and our cups.

And I can remember clearly now, how I felt after I wrote it, there's no point in denying anything. I remember sitting down for a long time, hardly moving, feeling as if my heart had slowed, was barely beating, having passion for nothing and no control.

So, it was there all right, it was the beginning of the preparation (probably the reason, for Christ's sake) for starting this; just a few simple lines, written in the middle of an ordinary day with the ease of changing a shirt while looking out, distracted, at a bird flying over the paddock.

But I had no idea, on that day, that within two weeks Charlie would be back and I would strike out, almost blindly, like a swimmer in deep water who lunges away from a dark shape ...

So there it is, here it is, here we are, coming home, but still a little way to go and who is that up ahead? Jesus! Slow down. Stand still. Do you want me to die trying to catch you?

When it rained in the city the water ran down the street outside our flat and at night the streetlights made it shine.

We'd been back for three weeks and in the flat for nearly two. Ruth chose it. She arrived with Claire and Jane only a few days after the boat.

The flat was in the middle of five others, all alike except for the colours. It was more like half a house, squashed looking and narrow with stairs leading up to a second floor and a small bedroom and balcony overlooking the street. Downstairs the kitchen opened into a little living room with a fireplace. The rent was cheap. Ruth liked the open fireplace and the wooden columns on the small verandah.

Charlie and Claire lived five miles away in a caravan park not far from the wharf. We saw them most days.

I bought a cheap car. We all had a fair bit of money from our final pay and we'd had a good couple of weeks: going to movies, the pub, playing pool and even taking Jane to the zoo. It had been good, but I knew Charlie was getting restless, and wasn't surprised when he said to me, 'Hey, I got some work. There's a dam going up, out in the hills, about eighty miles from here.'

'What are you driving?'

'Dozer, I think, maybe a bit of scraper work too. I ran into a bloke who works there, he set it up.'

The day they left it was raining and I heard the knock and opened the door and there was Charlie with Jane, shaking the rain from his hair and smiling as Claire came from the car, carrying a bag, crossing the street in her flowing way.

'We're on our way,' Charlie said. 'Got the billy on?'

We went inside and Ruth started to make coffee. I had a little fire going in the open fireplace. Claire stood with her back to it, rubbing her jeans and backside. Ruth came from the kitchen. 'Come and give me a hand, Joe.' I went in and we brought the coffee out. I handed a cup to Claire. She put it on the mantelpiece above the fire and said, 'Isn't the fire beautiful?'

'On days like this, yeah. Best thing in the world.'

It was easy to imagine Claire standing near any fire, moving with the same rhythm as quiet flames. You could picture her at all the small burning fires, outside a hut maybe, alone, waiting, bending to poke the coals. You wanted to say to her, 'Why do you stand there? Why is that calm look on your face as you watch the fire and wait?' You wanted to hear her say, 'When you're alone it's good to have a little fire.' But she would only ever say it with her eyes. When I saw her reach up for her cup of coffee above the fire it was easy to think of fires all across the country, a history of little glowing fires with women standing near them, night fires warming lonely women and it was easy to see a man come into the circle of light and warm himself near her fire and you wanted to say, 'Who are you, old man, and who is the woman near you? She has waited and kept the fire, who is she?'

Watching Claire made me think of people who come in from winter rain. I could see my father kick the coals with his boot and look out into the dark night, the fire glow showing the sad dream on his face that paused and then passed like a shadow over a paddock. I could say to him, 'What is it? Are you thinking of me and my friend, the son of your friend, the son of your old war mate? Do you wonder why we kill out on the water and come ashore to rip the land on the big machines? Is that what is on your face? Is it because you have watched the machines roll down the hills in another country and the bright blast of the bombs? Or are you thinking about the stern-faced priest in the little church with his clean robes and the solemn way he closes the Bible and folds the cloth over it while the wind bangs the windows?' You want to whisper: 'Don't be sad about the priest or me. Let him drink his wine and wipe the silver cup. Come with me and we'll drink together at the creek. We'll put our faces into the clear running water near the rock. But come with me later, not now. Because I am here with Claire, near the fire … and Charlie too, and Ruth.'

After they'd gone I'd put some more wood on the fire and Ruth came over to me and said, 'Let's go out tonight, have a meal, find a quiet place. Just us for a change.'

'All right.'

That afternoon I'd driven to the wharf. I told Ruth I was going to the wrecking yard to get a couple of bits I needed for the car, but I had no intention of doing that and followed the highway along the river, then turned off onto the coast road and drove down it until I crossed the old bridge and headed for Fisherman's Harbour. I don't know why; the season was over. Everyone had gone their own way. Martin had left a week earlier on his motorbike. When I asked him which way he was heading he said, 'Don't know really, I'm going east, cross the Nullarbor and see what happens from there.'

I couldn't see the boat. It wasn't at the old berth. Probably been slipped, in dry-dock somewhere for a bit of off-season maintenance.

I bought some chips at the fish shop, walked around for a while and chucked some scraps to the seagulls, then headed back to Ruth and I put my foot down going along the highway thinking about her.

We got ready and left the flat just after dark, walking.

'Let's just walk,' Ruth had said, 'and we'll find something, there are a few places around here.'

We walked up to the main street and along it. There was a little restaurant with lacy curtains pulled to the side of the windows and we could see candles burning inside on the tables. Ruth stopped and looked in, but we walked on and I said, 'What about the old pub on the corner?'

It was smoky inside near the bar and crowded but quieter at the back in the eating area.

We sat down and ordered. There was an old couple sitting at a table not far away. Our meal came.

'See that old couple sitting over there?' I said. Ruth turned, chewing, and looked across. It was the old woman I'd noticed first. She didn't seem hungry but the man did. I watched them and then looked over at the bar. Two men were sitting on stools. They leaned towards each other when they spoke.

'What were you saying about the old couple?' Ruth asked.

'No, it was nothing really. I was just watching them eat.'

The man had big, bony hands and he looked down at his plate all the time he was eating. The woman picked at her food. Earlier, I'd seen her walk to another table to get a salt shaker, smiling, walking back with it for him. This is what she loves now, I thought. She loves to see him happy with his food.

'Going to get a couple more drinks?' Ruth asked.

'Okay.'

I went over and waited near the two men at the bar. They had little piles of change in front of them. I took the drinks back and Ruth said, 'I'm going to have sweets too.'

'What'll you have?'

'How about a bit of you? You're pretty sweet.'

She slipped a shoe off under the table and rubbed her foot against my leg. I stood up. 'I'll find out what they've got.'

We had sweets and left, walked slowly along the street looking through shop windows.

'Look at these,' Ruth said. There were shoes on display. 'Look at that pair, aren't they gorgeous?'

We walked on. 'You want to have a coffee?' she asked.

'We can have one at home,' I said.

'Come on, don't be boring.' She pulled me in through the door of the bright little coffee shop.

Well, that's enough now, Sally, that's far enough for now. I don't know … there's probably more, but do you think I should really dig the whole thing up? Maybe I only imagined that you wanted me to scrape around there again. I'm not sure what it was with Ruth and me. It's easier just to sum it up simply now: After the fishing we had a little place in the city for a while, then Charlie and Claire left, Martin had gone and in the end, I suppose I knew I'd have to go too ... I still had a bit of money, that's true, but I couldn't stay there forever. I needed work. So I left as well, went up north again. Charlie had gone south, but I went north and got a job building a road, living in a camp.

If I'm honest (and I suppose I should be) I need to say that I didn't really paint the true picture for Ruth. I told her I was going up there to get work, that part of it was right ... I didn't really lie ... it's just that I don't think she ever realised it was over. I didn't tell her and maybe she expected that I'd be back or she'd come up ... but it was never going to be like that with us. I knew right at the start, I suppose ... I remember in the pub (the night of the fights) how Claire had come back from the dance floor, flushed, excited and she'd asked about Jane and sat down near me at the table in the crowded bar-room. She put her head right back and rolled it around; her neck was moist and she undid a button on her blouse and rubbed a hand under her chin, flicked her blouse open, relaxed, glowing and she looked at me and said, 'You could have stayed with Ruth, you know.'

'I know,' I'd said, and I think we both knew, at that moment, what would come between me and Ruth (it was like an axe falling down, smacking into the table, cold and hard through the noise and the smoke).

So ... that was it, bye bye Ruth. I didn't write to her, didn't hear anything for about a year until Claire told me at Charlie's funeral that she'd gone travelling overseas.

Anyway, it was a long time ago.

When Sally came home with Sonny she carried a bag of shopping in from the car and she was laughing about something that had happened at work. She helped me with the tea. We did it together, slicing up chicken and vegetables. I lit the fire. The weather had changed, it was colder and looked like rain in the north-west. Sally opened a bottle of wine and Sonny played outside until dark, scooting down the path on his skateboard.

'What have you been doing?' she asked me.

'Today?'

'Yeah.'

'Got some wood. Went for a swim.'

It rained later in the night, lashing across the roof, the wind making a roaring noise in the trees.

In the morning, when everyone had gone again and the house was empty, I went out with the ute to load the wood but kept going, turned onto the main road and drove to the cemetery. It's not far away. The graves looked clean and washed from the rain, the headstones glistened in the grey light. I walked over to my grandfather's grave and my grandmother's. Leaves and twigs were lying around. The peppermint trees were still bending and waving in the wind. I stood looking at the graves in the cold silence. Lizzie's grave was thirty miles away. When she died there was no cemetery here and she was buried in the next town. I'd been there a couple of times and seen the old stone with her name and the name of her baby. And Charlie was in the city with his little plaque. In the North, my father lay in the red earth, the baked earth under the blaze of sun and the Sturt's peas.

I walked away and drove the ute back and out to where the wood was scattered in the bush clearing, and started to load it on.

Late in the afternoon the weather settled. The wind dropped. Just before dark I went outside and the trees were still.

After tea I sat down to read a book and Sally looked up and said, 'Sonny, you'd better get ready for bed.'

She was on a chair with the newspaper, but she stood up and walked across the room to see what he was doing. I looked over at him sitting quietly on the floor. He had a pen and was tracing around some sort of puzzle in a kids' book.

Sally stood watching and waiting for him, then she turned to me and said, 'You're quiet tonight. How's the story going?'

'It's over.'

'What do you mean?'

'It's asleep. You were right. That part of it is over. The rest is up ahead.'

'So what will you do?'

'Just let it rest, I suppose. Rest in peace.'

'Be serious.'

I stood up and walked over and took both her hands. Sonny looked up. His face was saying, 'I don't know what you're doing.' I pulled Sally towards me and held her. Sonny hadn't moved. I could see him over Sally's shoulder. He had a funny little smile now and I looked away and out through the window at the high, beautifully bare moon.